T0147320

Whisper Power

And Other Stories

Myron C. Peterson

iUniverse, Inc.
Bloomington

Whisper Power
And Other Stories

iUniverse books may be ordered through booksellers or by contacting:

iUniverse
1663 Liberty Drive
Bloomington, IN 47403
www.iuniverse.com
1-800-Authors (1-800-288-4677)

Because of the dynamic nature of the Internet, any web addresses or links contained in this book may have changed since publication and may no longer be valid. The views expressed in this work are solely those of the author and do not necessarily reflect the views of the publisher, and the publisher hereby disclaims any responsibility for them.

Any people depicted in stock imagery provided by Thinkstock are models, and such images are being used for illustrative purposes only.

Certain stock imagery © Thinkstock.

ISBN: 978-1-4502-8734-0 (sc)
ISBN: 978-1-4502-8735-7 (ebook)
ISBN: 978-1-4502-8736-4 (dj)

Printed in the United States of America

iUniverse rev. date: 2/21/2011

Table of Contents

Part I

Whisper Power

Not to be free

Is not to be

And that's my simple song ....

"Is this the spaceship Titanic?" she asked.

"It's not a spaceship. It's the planet Earth," he answered.

"A spaceship, a planet, what's the difference? One is just larger than the other."

"Well, this is not the Titanic," he insisted. "It's the planet, Earth."

"I suppose you're certain. You look certain. Maybe my information was wrong. I don't know though," she added doubtfully.

"It's not the Titanic. this morning I have been walking in the fields. The early morning sun has made prisms on the budding bushes and the spring grass. I heard the crystal bells of a meadowlark singing. Actually there were several birds among the wildflowers. Their music matched the beauty of the blue lupin and the golden poppies.

"I felt warm and rich. Everything felt right. It was all as it should be."

"Remember, people were dining and dancing in the ballroom just before the Titanic hit an iceberg," she reminded him.

"I know we have problems, but there have always been problems. We have the people to solve them. All through history there have been voices crying out that we are headed for the rocks."

She looked around at the green rolling hills splashed with the yellow wild mustard and she listened for a while to the bees humming in the blossoms. Then she looked at him with penetrating eyes.

"Living here in your remote sanctuary, away from the people, are you really aware of reality?"

"I grew up with the people. I lived with the people and worked with the people. I have taught the people. And now I walk with nature, breathe in the fresh air and feel the warmth of the sun. I appreciate this garden of Eden in space. I see beauty everywhere and embrace it. Everyday I am grateful for this paradise we have been given and I want to dive into it, to tumble and roll in it, to be absorbed by it."

"When I first asked you if this was the spaceship Titanic and you said it was not, I thought you must be right. But now I think I may have asked the wrong person.

"You see," she continued, "I received a message from the spaceship Titanic. It came to me as a poem. I was starting to do some writing, and suddenly I was writing a poem. It crowded out all other thoughts. It seemed to be beamed from here. Listen, and I'll read it to you."

She reached into the bag that she carried on her arm and drew out a roll of parchment. Slowly she began to read:

"A message from the spaceship Titanic….

> This desecrated Earth cries out
> As Eden we destroy
> For we've become the Trojan horse
> And all the world's our Troy
>
> We rationalize our ruthlessness
> With reason we explain
> Why species we eliminate
> Why loss is really gain

Exterminating Everywhere
For comfort and for wealth
To make the planet more secure
And sterile for our health

Removing all the human race
From contact with the source
We want no risks and want no pain
And seek a carefree course

The challenge is for someone else
Results are guaranteed
And when somebody rocks our boat
We quickly show our greed

Compassion fades as wealth accrues
And more we grasp and save
Our things the master soon become
And we become the slave

Still heedlessly we rape the earth
And countless children sire
Then saddled by tremendous debts
We sink into the mire

Somewhere a land exists without
Polluted skies of gray
I'll load my loved ones in a boat
And quietly sail away.

When she had finished, she rolled up the parchment again and carefully put it back into her bag.

He watched her and gave a deep sigh.

"It appears to be a message from here alright," he said. "It points up some of our problems. But the writer seems to be giving up."

"That's why I came," she said. "I wanted to see things for myself. In fact I had to come. I couldn't get any of my writing done because these messages were crowding out my thoughts."

"Messages?" he asked. "Were there more than one?"

"Yes, there was another."

"Was it as depressing as the first?"

"I don't know if depressing is a word to describe it. I sense a kernel or hope in it, and some wisdom too. I think the sender knows it doesn't have to be this way on Earth."

"Now you have me curious," he said.

"Since you are interested, I may as well read you this one also," she said, as she again reached into her bag and drew out another roll of parchment.

To be secure I must give up
More freedom every day
I think I'll climb into my boat
And quietly sail away

And yet I know there's no escape
Unless I fly from here
And find a world where nations live
by love instead of fear

Irrational leaders guide their flocks
With fear the guiding light
Disarmed of faith they put their trust
In weapons for a flight

When leaders call their men to arms
They wave their flags with joy
And form long lines to pledge themselves
To kill a neighbor's boy

When we choose peace instead of fear
For arms there'll be no need
And then imprisoned brotherhood

Will at least be freed

We've produced great books of art
Fine music every year
but rational thought's eluded us
And still we're ruled by fear

Can we survive these savage ways
With such a thin veneer?
Will we at last destroy it all
With never ending fear?

"No wonder he wants to fly away," he said. "Your messenger's view of reality is very pessimistic. Do you think he will really try to fly away?"

"He, or she, probably can't," she answered. "In this present mood I think he would if he could, but there's really no escape. Perhaps the problems here are more serious than you imagine. My messenger doesn't seem to share your view that this is the Garden of Eden."

"And that is one of this problems, and the problem of so many others. Their negative views create negative results. Ideas gain strength and grow. I wonder who is sending these messages."

"That is one of the things I've come to find out," she said.

"I would certainly like to know that too," he nodded. "Maybe I can go along with you and try to find this frightened messenger. I think I can help."

"I would like that," she agreed. "I sense in you a kindred soul. It is as if I have known you before--perhaps in another life. Before we start, however, I would like to go back to your last remark about negative thinking. You think you know about negative thinking, but do you really? Such thinking is very hard to comprehend. If you are going to help the message sender you must understand what you are doing.

"I think that one of my stories will let you test yourself. It is called The Plot."

For the third time she reached into her bag and drew out a manuscript.

"You have an amazing bag," he said. "It is like a personal library."

She smiled and began to read:

The seven members of the discussion group settled back in their chairs, each one holding his newspaper clipping in his hand. Jerry Bensen, the leader, pushed the coffee pot and cookies to the end of the table and sat down to join the others.

"It looks like everyone is prepared," he said. "I see you all holding your clippings and I imagine it was very difficult to select the most impressive story when so many things are happening and being reported every day. Let's start with you Mrs. Johnson, Martha. Would you like to tell us about your story?"

Martha nodded, her face blooming with a radiant smile. "The most impressive story to me was the one about the mother and father in Chicago who deliberately smothered their little boy because they were splitting up and neither of them wanted him."

"That was terrible," Sonja Hellman agreed. "Imagine people doing things like that."

"Why did you choose such a horrible story?" Jerry Bensen asked.

"It was a big story. It was on all the T.V. news too," Martha said, defensively.

"But very negative!" Jerry added.

"Who else has a story?"

"I have one similar to Martha's," Bill Roberts said. "It is the story of a man who was convicted of drowning his wife and her son, his step-son, in order to collect their insurance. He took them out to sea and sank the boat."

"How terrible!" Sonja Hellman repeated again. "How can their be such people?"

"I am surprised you have chosen such negative stories," Jerry said. "did you read everything?"

"We chose the main stories in the paper," Bill protested. "The assignment was to choose the most impressive stories."

"I have one that is not about murder," George Adams said. "Mine is about the politicians in Washington who were arrested for taking bribes during the F.B.I. investigation. Corruption is rampant in Washington. Everyone must have his hand out."

Jerry turned to Mary Cooper who had been patiently waiting her turn. "Do you have an impressive story?" he asked.

"My story has a picture with it," she said, holding up her paper. "See all the unemployed workers standing in line for their relief checks. The lines are getting longer every day."

Continuing around the group, Jerry nodded to Barbara Bailey.

"The story that impressed me the most was the one about the hijackers who have seized an airliner with ninety-four passengers and are demanding the release of their comrades who attempted to assassinate the president. It's a terrible situation."

Don Radcliffe had a story about racial discrimination in the financial industries, and Brad Scott's story was about how inflation was ruining those retired on fixed incomes.

"How do you all feel about these stories? Do you think we have chosen the most impressive ones?" Jerry asked.

"Well, I have another one," Martha said. "It is about the West side rapist who has attached sixteen women in the last three months and has still not been caught."

"Negative! All negative!" Jerry shouted. "Don't you all feel depressed? Isn't anything good and positive happening?"

"Not much," George Adams said. "Everything's going to the dogs or coming apart at the seams."

"It can't be all bad!" Jerry insisted. "There are all kinds of people doing all kinds of things every day. How could we exist if everything were bad?"

"It's pretty bad," Sonja said. "People killing their children, raping, taking bribes…"

The others were all nodding. Their faces wore frowns.

"Stop! Don't you see what you're doing? You're making it worse by believing it is that way. You are creating this reality by your negative thoughts and beliefs!"

"How can you think positively about it when all these terrible things are happening?" Don Radcliffe asked. "You can't be like an ostrich and stick your head in the sand."

"You can't make things better by pretending they don't exist," Brad said. "You have to recognize reality."

"But this isn't reality!" Jerry said. "Don't you see? This is just a small part of what is happening."

"You must read different papers than we do," George said.

"No, I read the same papers, and I listen to the same T.V. and I know most of the stories are very negative."

"Almost all of them," Mary said.

"You'd have to read all the small print if you expected to find anything positive," George added.

"It must be a plot," Jerry said. "It is some kind of a plot to destroy us. Someone has gained control of the news media and is using it against us. Someone knows that we will be destroyed by negative thinking.

"Remember how people used to be cheerful and optimistic about everything? There wasn't anything we couldn't do. Everywhere there was confidence and we could laugh at misfortunes. What has happened? We are being undermined. Yes, and the press is the instrument that is being used! We've been worrying about nuclear bombs when we were under attach from the airways!"

"I don't know how it all came about," Sonja nodded," but things are certainly pretty bad."

That night Jerry couldn't sleep. He was obsessed with his discovery. At least it was all clear. The danger was everywhere. People must be alerted. The government must be made aware of this war that was going on. He Jerry Bensen, must lead the crusade.

He must contact his congressman and senators. He had a campaign plan that had to be successful. The negative forces had to be stopped!

"But who do you think is doing this, Mr Bensen?" Senator Bradbury asked. "Who has infiltrated the media and is using it so successfully?"

"Sir, I don't know who they are. They could be communists, fascists, some negative religious group, forces from outside the planet or some other unknown group. Someone or something is seizing control of people's minds and destroying us with negative thoughts. Their disciples and the advocates of negative thinking must be stopped."

"If you are right, how do you suggest we begin this counter offensive? How can we detect and stem the influences of these people?"

"Form an investigating committee. You will soon detect the purveyors of negative thinking. Those who keep telling us how bad things are will be the leaders of the plot."

Jerry Bensen was a very persuasive speaker, and soon committees were formed in both houses of congress and the investigations were under way. And, surprisingly enough, the news was getting better.

Jerry did not rest with this accomplishment, but continued to travel around the country doing his part. Lecturing to women's groups and business clubs he constantly told of the terrible plot that was destroying the nation.

One day Martha Johnson and Sonja Hellman were passing a news stand and they counted three different magazines with Jerry Bensen's picture on the cover.

"Jerry is really getting famous," Martha said. "Everybody in the country must know who he is by now."

"Last week I saw him on the this Week show on T.V.," Sonja agreed. "Do you every watch the T.V. talk shows? I hear he's been on several of them."

"I saw him on the marty Dill show a couple of weeks ago. He said that there were conspirators everywhere and the negatives were destroying the country."

"On the evening news last night it said Jerry was being invited to Washington. He's getting up there!"

And indeed Jerry Benson was being noticed by Washington. He was invited to talk to the committee he had asked congress to set up, the committee to investigate the negative plot.

However, when he arrived at the capital city his reception was a little surprising. Instead of being asked to address the committee, as he was accustomed to doing when he was invited to meet with an organization, he was ushered to a seat facing the men. The committee members were sitting on a raised platform, a group of judges peering down on him. He felt intimidated. They were giants and he was a dwarf sitting in a hole.

"Jerry Bensen, you have been going around the country warning of a negative plot," one of the men said.

"And you have caused this committee to be formed to investigate these charges," another said.

"And we have been investigating," a third added.

"You have warned us that the negative stories in the media were a conspiracy to undermine this country," the first continued.

"That we could tell the enemy by the negative propaganda he was dispersing. The conspirators in this plot could be identified by their constant barrage of stories about how terrible everything is in this country," the second continued.

"And we have come to the conclusion," the third added, "that you are the leader of this plot. For what could be more negative that you traveling all over the country telling us how bad the media is and how we are destroying ourselves." the third added.

"It can't be all that bad," the first said.

"There are all kinds of people doing all kinds of things every day," the second said.

"How could we exist if everything were that bad?" the third asked.

"For the good of the country, and to promote more positive thinking, you must be removed from society," the first said.

Jerry looked at the committee with a dazed look. His head was swimming, his eyes glazed.

"They've won," he whispered. "The country is ruined."

All the judges nodded in agreement as the first said firmly, "There's the proof!" \

When the story was finished there were several minutes of silence as she rolled up the parchment and placed it back in the bag with the others.

"Did you read me this to warn me?" he asked.

"If you need a warning, accept it," she answered. "the only way to deal with negative thought is to replace it with positive thinking."

"Can we begin to look for the sender of the messages?" he asked.

"Wait! Wait!" she answered. "Another message is coming through."

Quickly setting down her bag she drew out a blank sheet of note paper and a pen. Then, after staring at the tall Eucalyptus trees in the distance and turning her head as if to listen to an unheard voice, she began to write:

> Some try to make me hate myself
> And undermine my pride
> Because my ways are not the same
> They want to make me hide
>
> They may harm me physically
> And they may even kill
> But force me to destroy myself
> This they never will
>
> For I know I have always been
> And I will always be
> And though my body can be chained
> My soul is always free

Slowly she laid down the pen and studied the paper carefully.

"Is that all?" he asked.

"yes," she answered quietly.

"And is it from the same person?" he asked

"I am certain they are all from the same person, but this message shows courage."

"And some wisdom," he added. "This one is a deep thinker."

"Indeed," she agreed. "I must find this sender, this source of ideas."

"We need a direction finder," he said. "Can you home in on that last message? Is it like a radio broadcast? Is it stronger in one direction?"

"A telepathic message is not like that. It just comes. But I seem to sense that it is coming from the West. The message was very strong, so I think we are very close."

"The West would be over by the shore," he said. "The ocean is just over that hill."

"Then let us quickly walk over there," she said.

"What will you do when you find the one you seek?" he asked.

"I shall read him my prophecy," she said.

"Your prophecy?" he puzzled.

"Yes, prophecy. The prophecy that can be. I have written it as a story."

"How will that help this troubled messenger?"

"When you hear the prophecy your question will be answered. I feel this is what I must do."

The two new friends began their short walk to the shore. As they climbed to the top of the hill they looked down on a small bay where the ocean water was breaking gently against the narrow, sandy beach that was still damp from the outgoing tide.

Two tiny sail boats were tied to mooring buoys out in the water and a small, but tidy, fishing pier led out into the bay.

At first it appeared that the area was deserted except for the tiny shore birds running along the edge of the water in search of food and a few gulls hang gliding on outstretched wings over the sea. However, as the two searchers came closer to the beach they saw a solitary human figure sitting on the sand near the pier.

It appeared to be a girl with her back resting against a large rock and her knees drawn up in front of her. Her clasped hands were resting on her knees, and her chin was pressed against her hands.

"Do you think she is asleep?" he asked.

"No," she answered. "The girl is lost in thought. Her mood is sad and she is contemplating the meaning of life. She is thinking very deeply."

Suddenly the girl looked up with startled eyes as she saw the two visitors. She got half up and then settled back to the sand again.

"Oh!" she exclaimed. "I thought I was along."

"You were," she answered. "We have invaded your privacy and we apologize."

"It's alright," the girl said. "It's a public beach."

"To tell you the truth, it was not an accident," she explained. "I received a message from one in urgent need and I thought you might be the sender."

"It must be someone else you are looking for," the girl said. "I have sent no messages--not even in a bottle thrown into the sea. I've just been sitting here thinking."

"About climbing into one of those boats out there and quietly sailing away?" she asked.

"That's unreal," the girl said with wide eyes and a half smile.

"It was what you were thinking," she said smiling. And she continued, "For I know I have always been, and I will always be; and though my body can be chained, my soul is always free."

"I don't believe it!" the girl said.

"I've had enough experiences to be older," the girl answered. "And faced more problems than many people twice my age."

"You have lost someone close to you?" she asked.

"Yes, the one I loved the most is now gone. Death is so final."

"And there were other problems?" he asked, breaking his silence.

"I thought I had a terminal illness, but now the doctors tell me I will live. I will recover."

"Such news should make you happy," she said, "but still you are sad. "After such experiences we realize that things can never again be the same."

"At such times you review all human values," he added. "You evaluate all that is important."

"And the world can be very depressing," the girl added. "How petty things seem. How blind and selfish people can be. Too many people act with little concern about the consequences and they spend their precious days fighting about things that do not matter."

"It can be discouraging," he agreed. "It doesn't pay to think too much about certain things."

"But we are thinking beings," the girl said.

"You are the one!" she said. "It is you who have been sending me messages, and now I have one for you."

Again she reached into her bag and pulled out a scroll. This one, however, had been tied with a green ribbon and was held by a golden seal. With a nod she handed it to the amazed girl.

"Break the seal and unroll it," she instructed her. "The message is for you."

With some hesitation the girl accepted it, holding it with both hands as if it were a fragile egg. Then, with a fingernail she broke the golden seal, unrolled the parchment and softly read the message aloud:

> I want to make them understand
> Their lives they can retrieve
> The road to peace lies in ourselves
> If we can just believe
>
> We will have peace when we choose peace
> And we renounce the sword
> No government can people trust
> For peaceable accord
>
> We cannot listen to a voice
> That speaks of ancient hate
> We can't commit inhuman acts
> To suit a national state
>
> And we can save our biosphere
> This tiny planet Earth
> By appreciating all
> And knowing all have worth
>
> Everyone we must accept
> Whatever he might be
> No one has the mind or eye
> To know what God can see

For everything upon this earth
With purpose plays its role
And everything is just one part
Of universal whole

The most important thing to us
Is what we all believe
For miracles are made by faith
That human minds conceive

When she had finished reading, the girl looked up with a trace of tears in her eyes.

"Thank you," her voice said softly.

"It was not the only message I have brought you. I also have a prophecy.

Reaching once more into her bag she drew out the largest scroll of all.

"Is that the prophecy that can be?" he asked.

"That is the one," she answered. "It is called <u>Whisper Power</u>."

Everyone reclined on the soft, warm sand and even the seagulls settled down along the shore. They stood in a group facing the reader while their feet were gently washed by the undulating water.

The voice of the reader had the musical quality of crystal chimes touching gently together in the breeze, and in the sky about the clouds gathered in little white patches ready to illustrate the story.

He and the girl listened intently, for they did not want to miss any part of the prophecy that can be.

WHISPER POWER

"There's something going on Anna, I just know it. At work the bosses are huddled together talking in whispers. They all have worried looks on their faces."

"Government people are always worried. I've never seen them when they didn't think doomsday was tomorrow."

"I know, but this seems different. Today going to work on the supertram Jim Clark sat next to me. He works in Military Services, and he said the high brass were in meetings all day. Some of the top industrialists flew in from all over the world. He said the office was like a small United Nations."

"Oh Bill, you know how those people thrive on secrecy and games--makes them feel important. They're just cooking something up to increase their profits. You've worked for them long enough to know how their lives are just one crisis after another."

"I know! I know! but this isn't an ego trip for anyone. You can tell. This time it's different. You can feel it. Even when I was walking home from the tram stop I could feel it."

"Now that you mention it, that reminds me of a strange thing that happened to me at the market. A group of women were talking together at the back of the store, and while I was browsing through the vegetable department a girl came over to me and asked me what I thought of the Mid-African war."

"What did you tell her?"

"Since she was a complete stranger to me, and I thought it was funny she would come up to me just like that, I didn't say much. I think I said something like we had a government to worry about that."

"What did she do then?"

"She just smiled and said thanks and went back to the group."

"That's something like what happened to me at the tram stop. A group of men were talking and one of them came over to me and asked if I were a government worker. When I told him I was, he asked me if I thought the Mid-Africa war was in our national interest. I told him it didn't pay for government workers to express opinions on such things. I told him I just did my job and didn't mix in politics."

"Did he give you an argument?"

"No, Anna. He just smiled and nodded and went back over to talk to the other men."

That night Bill Mentor had trouble getting to sleep, and all night he tossed and felt partially awake. It was as if strong and conflicting thought waves were probing into his consciousness. His mind was a neutral bastion besieged by powerful, alien ideas. In the morning he was more exhausted that when he had gone to bed.

"Anna," he said at breakfast, "do you believe in extra sensory thought projection? Do you believe someone can think something so hard that the idea reaches into the minds of other people? All night I felt like I was being invaded. I hardy slept at all."

Anna looked at Bill with dismay, "You too?"

"Didn't you sleep well either?"

"I dreamed I was in the middle of a huge flower field and the petals were closing all around me. I could hear thousands of people chanting and singing. It was almost like a religious ritual that I couldn't understand."

"This whole thing is beginning to scare me," Bill shuddered. "Maybe it is connected with all those meetings at work. Do you think an alien force could be using telepathy to gain control? One person couldn't muster that much brain power, could he?"

"I don't think one person could influence very many people over a large area. Sometimes if they are all gathered together in a stadium or auditorium a lot of people seem to be brought into unit thinking in some almost hypnotic way. A speaker on a television screen seems to have a great influence, but there is eye to eye contact and a voice factor there. No I can't see how one person could exercise that much control over thought. Besides, we were mostly troubled at night. The person using mind control would have to sleep sometime."

"Maybe we are just scaring ourselves. I think we should forget the whole thing."

Bill's determination to put all disturbing ideas out of his mind worked for a short time, but as he started to work the same worries crept back into his consciousness. People on the street were walking in groups. Everyone seemed to be looking anxiously around. The air was electrified. It was as if the whole city was waiting for a titanic football game.

However, the television news reports were the usual routine happenings. There were some accidental deaths, minor thefts, and the usual raids of counter raids by the mid African combatants. More supplies were being sent to the favored side and relief was being provided to the refugees. The only unusual item was the weather news. The unusually mild winter and spring had enabled gardeners to grow an abundance of flowers. Even the wild flowers were more prolific. Airline pilots reported seeing fields of poppies growing as far north as the Arctic Circle. Some passengers had seen the orange patches in mountain valleys surrounded by snow.

Although nothing was being said publicly, the secret meetings continued and Bill watched uneasily as he worked at his desk in the government office. It was to seek relief from the mounting tension that at lunch time he decided to go downtown to a new ultramodern restaurant rather than eat in the government cafeteria. The prices were higher at the restaurant, but there were padded booths and soft music. After such a hectic night Bill felt he needed a more restful atmosphere.

As he entered the dining room he noticed once again a group of men talking earnestly with hushed voices. They were seated at a booth, and since the booth next to them was empty Bill had an opportunity to sit close enough to do a little eavesdropping. He was determined to listen in on some of that conversation and find out if they were discussing the thing that seemed to concern everyone and about which he knew nothing. The way everyone was so secretive was giving him a complex.

There were four men in the booth and their low voices were drowned out by the background music and the clatter of dishes from the kitchen. However, after a while Bill's ears began to tune out the many disturbances and he began to pick up some of the conversation.

"It's ridiculous!" one of the men was saying. "Here in this age of space travel and long life we are still divided into hostile camps. Here we are still grouped into separate petty states fighting like gangs over scraps of territory on this planet. All we've accomplished socially is to cover our gang activities with an acceptable veneer."

"That's not a new idea," another voice answered. "People have been saying that for centuries. For generations scientists have been saying we've advanced far more rapidly technologically than we have socially. We still are primitives!"

"When you say we, who are you talking about? Do you know anyone who wants to fight in a war? Even the soldiers don't want to fight. Look at the Mid-African war. Nobody wants it!"

"yes, but some people way it is necessary."

"Where did they get that idea? They are just mouthing the propaganda put out by the government. You don't see our leaders over there fighting. If it were like it was in the middle ages when the kings and nobles led their troops into battle there would be a lot fewer wars. That has been our modern mistake-letting out leaders make war without having to lead their troops. Today they make war from bomb proof shelters."

"Wait a minute," a voice interrupted. "They still had wars in the middle ages when the nobles led the fighting."

"But those leaders didn't face weapons of total annihilation. I doubt if you'd find leaders willing to head the troops today."

The voices were rising now and everyone was talking at once. It was difficult to tell who was saying what.

"It's about time the soldiers all over the world realize, whey they are ordered to invade another country, the enemy is the one who put them in the front lines and ordered them to kill or be killed--if not by the enemy, by their superiors in the rear," a voice said. "The real enemy isn't the soldier they are facing. He's just some poor guy in the same boat they are in."

"You have to ask yourself who can gain by it all. That will mark the enemy. None of the soldiers on either side can do anything but lose."

"it's really not much different from the human sacrifices of the Aztecs. They sacrificed young people out of fear. They thought civilization would be destroyed by the gods if they didn't kill all these victims. They even dressed the young men up and made heroes of them before sending them to the sacrificial altar. Aren't we doing the same thing? We tell our people we have to sacrifice all these people in a war on some foreign battleground in order to preserve our way of life."

"Every government believes these things and fears other countries will destroy them. There never has been a way for the people all over the world to break out of this system."

"Yet, whenever the young people from different countries get together they enjoy each other's company, make friends and are happy together. None seem to covet another's country or want to take things away from their neighbors. They aren't burglars and thugs."

Suddenly one of the men jumped up exclaiming that they were late, and all four hastily rushed to the cashier.

Bill gave a deep sigh. He certainly didn't learn anything here, except he believed some the talk had bordered on treason. Saying the enemy was he one who sent the soldiers into combat! That, after all, was the government! These people weren't realistic. Even if they were right about government propaganda stirring people up to fight, if other people believed it and attacked you, you would have to fight and defend yourself. The whole conversation was a real disappointment and didn't shed any light on the apparent alarm that was sweeping the country. It certainly had not helped that deep and unexplainable feeling of panic he felt.

"It's as if my conscious can hardly suppress my subconscious. Maybe I'm losing my mind. Maybe it's part of this Mid-African war. Could our enemies have discovered a new weapon. Oh God, we may all be driven out of our minds!"

"Have you walked in the park, Bill?"

The sudden sound of his name scattered his thoughts.

"What's the matter, Bill? You look lost."

Bill looked up to see his friend Jim Clark standing right beside the booth.

"I'm sorry, Jim, I didn't see you come in. I was just thinking about all this hush-hush mystery stuff. I think it's driving me nuts!"

"I was feeling nervous myself," Jim agreed. "That's why I thought I'd walk through the park on my way to lunch. Have you been in the park lately?"

"Not for months, why?"

"The flowers! I couldn't believe the number of flowers in the park. There are usually a few beds around the fountain and at the entrance, and the rest of the park is grass and trees. This year the whole place is a riot of color. There are golden poppies coming up all over. Somebody must have scattered a lot of seed.

"And the same people must have been over on eighth street too--you know, where they have all those window boxes. I don't usually notice those things, but the orange color was so bright it leaped right our at me. The poppies are all in bloom. Bill, I tell you this city is changing. People are planting more flowers this year.

"Of course, working in that office all the time you don't see the changes around you. Usually I just walk directly to the office from the tram stop, and I'm always thing about some problem."

"I know," Bill nodded. "Down at the government office I've been a cave dweller, a miner deep in the earth. I don't think I'm even in the mainstream of life anymore. In face I'm beginning to think I'm on the verge of an identity crisis."

"I feel pretty much out of things too." Jim agreed. "The good times I can relate to were things that happened years ago; although I suppose people are still having fun today. Somebody must be.

"I especially feel like an outsider when I see all these groups of people whispering together an I see people rushing in and out of conferences that I can't participate in. It appears as if we live in a time when momentous things are taking place and I don't even know what's going on. I'm just a catalyst helping to make things function without any place in the real picture.

"I'm beginning to wonder if people really are acting different than usual," Bill said. "Are they really whispering together, or just engaged in their usual conversations? Are we beginning to suspect some conspiracy without supporting facts? Jim, maybe we are the ones who are the problem. We may have some guilt complex--we at the government office. It could be the long unpopular Mid-Africa war. After all our work helps to make it all possible. Maybe it's working on us subconsciously and we're suffering from paranoia. It could all be in our minds. Maybe we've cracked!"

When he returned to work Bill found his efficient sanctuary in a state of confusion. Two of the clerks did not come back from lunch and the communications operator had abruptly quit his job. Everyone else was trying to do the extra work required to keep things going, and Bill had to take over part of the phone network along with his other duties. To make matters worse his mind was more cluttered than ever. His thoughts kept jumping from one thing to another and his concentration quotient sank to almost zero.

However, while at the phone center he did pick up a bit of interesting information. A group of marchers protesting the Mid-African war had streamed right through the capitol building, down the aisle where the national assembly was in session, across the speaker's platform and out the near doors. No one had any idea how they had slipped past the guards, and the representatives were furious to think no warning alarm had been given. Fortunately the demonstrators were unarmed and peaceful. They were just a line of silent marchers carrying signs.

Because of this astounding breach in security systems there was a cry of outrage from the legislators and demands that the administration and the army explain what was going on. The administration, in answer to the alarm, had agreed to have the minister of defense go on national television at 6:00 p.m. to answer the charges of incompetence and to calm any outbreaks of hysteria among the people.

"That is one speech everyone will listen to," Bill said to himself. "I hope it isn't just a propaganda release. If I'm going to retain my sanity, I'm going to have to hear something meaningful to me."

Anna and Bill were restless with anticipation when the great clock in the hall chimed 6:00 p.m.

"I'll bet he won't say anything important," Bill said pessimistically. "Every time I think I'll finally learn what's happening in this country all I hear is the same old stuff. Nobody seems to care about the truth. They just want to convince everyone they are right."

"You won't hear anything if you don't stop talking," Anna interrupted. "There's Jeffery Downs now."

"Looking as insincere as ever! But look who else is there. It looks as if the whole cabinet is standing beside him. Maybe they are going to have one of their heart to heart panel discussion."

The program started with the playing of martial music by the army band. Then the glee club stepped forward and sang the great rally song:

> Come on and follow me
> And we will set them free
> And we will build a great new world society

Come on and give a cheer
That everyone can hear
Who wants to rule mankind
With prejudice and fear.

'though sacrifices great
Will always be our fate
Don't hesitate
Come on and follow me!

"That is a great and inspiring song," Anna said.

"Every country has one similar, but it just gets them into trouble," Bill said.

Anna frowned and was about to say something, but the speech on the television had started.

"Citizens everywhere," the defense minister began. "As you know there has been much concern lately over the Mid-African war and the things your government has been compelled to do in the interest of peace, justice and our own national security. There are some among our countrymen who believe there is an easy and simple solution to the complex dangers that confront us. Their native simplicity could easily bring ruin to us all. Therefore, I have invited the leadership cabinet to join with me in an informative panel as to why.....as to why....ahem...."

The voice of Jeffery Downs seemed to fade. He put his hand to his mouth and coughed slightly.

"May I have a glass of water?" he asked meekly.

A hand pushed a glass of water across the screen. Jeffery Downs reached out and took it from the table. After slowly sipping some of the water he carefully replaced the glass on the table, straightened his tie and continued.

"Excuse me. We are here to.......a ....give you all, my fellow citizens, that is my fellow citizens of the world, what you all want. It is what we all want. And what is that? PEACE!"

Suddenly he broke into a joyful smile and shouted the word again, "PEACE!"

He continued, "And how does this world peace begin? You all know! You've been talking about it for weeks. You've been whispering it in ...ah...seditious meetings. Who among you does not know the twenty-first century pledge?"

"What's he talking about, Anna?" Bill asked, shaking his head.

"I don't know, but this isn't according to plan. You can tell that. Look at the cabinet members. A minute ago they looked angry, like they were going to grab Downs, but now they all have those silly grins on their faces. They look like they are high on something."

"What in the hell is going on?" Bill jumped to his feet.

On the television screen the defense minister was tearing up his speech. "Let's recite the pledge together," he insisted, turning to the panel.

Together they chanted: "I realize, as a member of the human race on a small planet, I have a responsibility to all. I believe all people want to live in peace. Neighbors do not want to kill their neighbors. I will accept this new world and not listen to the voices of hate or ancient territorial claims. My only fight will be defensive, defending and protecting if attacked. I will not be the aggressor and will never kill men, women or children in another country. And I will not support the prosecution or persecution of anyone in my own country for beliefs different from my own. I will seek truth, be compassionate and respect all life on this planet."

Turning again to face the camera, defense minister Jeffery Downs stated triumphantly, "Today the majority of people in every country on earth is repeating this pledge. The Mid-African war is over. Peace has won."

"They got to him!" Bill exclaimed with disbelief. "They do have a secret weapon! They've mastered telepathy!"

"Maybe if enough people really want and believe something it becomes that way," Anna said calmly. "Maybe it's not a weapon at all. It may have always been that way. Perhaps it is called prayer."

On the television there was pandemonium. The music was playing and everyone was starting to sing. The music seemed to be coming form outside also, and even from next door.

Bill rushed to the window and threw back the drapes. Everywhere there was an overwhelming sight. It was New Year's Eve in Time

Square, the Rose Parade, or a California valley in the springtime. The streets were filled with rivers of people, and they were carrying and throwing bouquets of flowers. The blossoms and petals were landing everywhere--orange flowers, golden poppies.

On the television screen too, there were poppies everywhere, and all the people were laughing and hugging each other. And they were all singing! From the streets came more singing. Everyone was singing in unison in the streets and on the screen. The whole world seemed to be singing:

> See the fields of golden poppies
> Rivaling the sun
> Wear a brilliant, golden poppy
> We will be as <u>one.</u>
>
> Poppies grow in mass with freedom
> Mountains to the sea
> Wear the peaceful, golden poppy
> Fear no enemy.
>
> Find your gold within the poppy
> See the beauty here
> Join in tribute to our planet
> Love will banish fear.

Anna looked at Bill and he was singing. She smiled broadly, for she was singing herself. They looked at each other, happy and puzzled. They knew all the words.

When the story ended there were several minutes of silence before anyone spoke. Then, the girl raised up on her elbow and looked at the reader, but she saw only the sandy beach and the seagulls wading in the surf along the shore.

"Where did she go?' she asked.

"I imagine she left the way she came," he answered. "She seems to appear or vanish at will."

"It would have been nice to talk with her some more," the girl said. "I wonder why she left so abruptly?"

"I guess her mission here was finished," he said. "She had been doing some writing, but messages kept interrupting her thoughts. I think she's gone back to work."

"She seems to think I was sending the messages."

"I think so too," he agreed. "When she received them she thought our Earth was the spaceship Titanic."

"I don't think they will be that depressing again," the girl smiled.

"Well, I must go along too," he smiled back. "I will continue walking and singing my song."

As he climbed over the hill the words drifted back along the beach and out over the sea to where the two bobbing boats seemed to nod in agreement.

> Not to be free
> Is not to be
> And that's my simple song.
>
> Don't try to pour me
> In a mold
> Where I do not belong.
>
> People living everywhere
> Want to go their way
> Without big brother telling them
> What to do or say.
>
> So come along
> And sing with me
> Not to be free
> Is not to be.....

Part II

Visions of the Future

From the mirrors of time
the ideas come.
With pens
we try to freeze them
and hold them
in an artificial present tense
that does not exist.
We create a reality
from reflected images
of a past as we believe it to have been
and of a future
as we imagine it will be.
All we see are visions
in the mirrors of time.

As You Believe

"He's the most difficult man to convince of anything I've ever seen! He wouldn't believe the sky was blue without some spectrum analysis. I could run out of the house screaming fire and he'd say, 'Calm down and analyze the facts. Was there visual evidence? Did you actually smell smoke? Was there an unusual amount of heat?' The whole place could burn down before he'd be ready to take action."

"As his wife, you know John better than anyone else, but as his sister I'd have to agree with you. When we were growing up he was the same way. He was never willing to accept any thing as true without a mountain of proof.

"He admits it himself--says he learned his lesson young when the neighborhood kids used to tease him. One day the boy next door told him there was a bear in the garage. John thought it was true and ran into the house screaming.

"Of course everyone tried to tell him the boy was just kidding him, but John wouldn't believe them. He was too scared to go outside. Finally, Dad took him by the hand and led him to the garage telling him all the while that it was all a joke, that the boys liked to tease, and that he shouldn't be afraid.

"With much soft talk he coaxed John into opening the garage door. That was when they both had a traumatic experience. With a snarl a huge brown bear lunged out and chased them both back to the house.

"No one ever knew where that bear came from or how it got into our garage. The neighborhood kids swore they had just made up the story. They were as scared as John. However, John was convinced that it was his own fault that the bear was in the garage. He said it came from his imagination and it was there because he believed it was. I don't think he ever recovered from that incident because since then he's been cautious about everything. He's still very careful about his beliefs."

"I can understand a child believing a thing like that, but John's an educated man now. Surely he still doesn't think that way."

"Maybe he doesn't. I don't know. To demand proof of everything has become a habit with him. He can drive you crazy. However, I do think it all started with that bear incident."

While the women at home discussed John Sperus, he was busy at work doing the thing he loved most, scientific research. Although he was enthusiastic about his work and spoke eagerly of his achievements, he rarely talked about his personal life or himself, and never seemed to discuss his true feelings with anyone--not even his wife. His life was a sober, sensible, dull existence. Since he never indulged in gossip or ridicule, never teased or joked about anything, and absolutely never took a drink, his close friends were few. Yet, although he impressed everyone as a serious and business-like person, deep down below this calm, highly efficient facade lived a chained fear. It moved in and out of his consciousness like a shadow in a fog, and flared and flickered like a fire, burning on the edges of his thought with always the threat of bursting into a conflagration. It was a fear that John Sperus felt could turn the whole world, indeed the entire universe, into a holocaust.

If the people around him could read his thoughts he'd be on a psychiatrist's couch or in a padded cell within minutes, but John knew this and was very careful and exact in what he did, and he constantly covered his inner struggles. Like waters of a turbulent, wild river, his inner feelings had to be dammed.

So far the massive control system he had developed had worked very well. He was thirty-two years old and his every moment was as technically controlled as a nuclear generating station. There had been no run away reactions or perilous breakdowns.

"Whenever a problem requires careful analysis without hasty decisions, I give it to John," his boss said. "Some people may count to ten before giving a definite answer, but John counts to one hundred.

It sounds ridiculous, and I sometimes wonder how we accomplish anything, yet, since he took over the science research this company has mushroomed into the most advanced business of its kind in the country. When John says something will work or develop in a certain way, it always does. He may take his time, but he's been one hundred percent right. His department has grown so large that he's now working on a plan to train highly intelligent students to carry on the advanced research. He says, and he has me convinced, that this is the way to even greater future accomplishments. He talks enthusiastically of potential discoveries by intelligent, imaginative young people. These organizational plans are taking him a while to develop because he is so damn cautious--wants to be sure any discoveries are used for the benefit rather than the detriment of people. As I've said, he's slow, but has a perfect record in achieving his goals."

It wasn't long after he had given this picture of John Sperus to his board of directors that his boss decided it was time to give John the needed push.

"You've been working on this training curriculum a long time John, what are you waiting for? Let's begin the inter views. You keep saying you must be sure you get the right people for your project, but haven't indicated how you will find them."

"I think I'm ready, but we must be very careful. We want people with social awareness as well as high intelligence. We have to consider everything. A kind, understanding, social minded person, even with the best of intentions, may ruin everything because of a lack of discipline and real intelligence."

"That's pretty vague, John. What do you mean by real intelligence?"

"First, I think each person should be able to see the broad relationship between things and must be able to generalize ideas. Second, he must be able to see the ultimate consequences of what he does. Third, he must have the mental discipline to stick to his idea without wavering. Fourth, he must have the will and determination to see that a thing is used only for the general welfare and not for private gain. For you see the knowledge that I will impart to each one will be powerful and give him fantastic potentials."

"You sound like a god about to give us the gift of fire."

"Each of the discoveries may be like that. With these people I intend to open the windows of the universe. Each one will have his own particular field of knowledge and will become the world's genius in it."

"Whatever you have planned in that computer brain," his boss said, "let's get on with it. Time is important too."

At last the great quest for John's chosen people began. The drag lines were thrown out to the universities and major industries. Many curious young scholars and ambitious intellectuals were drawn in for interviews and preliminary examinations.

One of the first to reply was Ella Morrison, an award winning social studies major who needed a job in order to earn enough money to continue her education. On a fateful day Ella read the ad and walked into a fanatical world where fanciful people planned without humor and worked without diversion.

John Sperus was truly impressed with Ella's transcripts and records. Here was a student whose college work was brilliant--a student who had never known failure. Ella had met many diverse challenges with triumphant success. She also seemed to be endowed with a social consciousness and a keen awareness of the problems of others. She was a person with a rare combination of abilities.

"This is the one," he said to himself. "She will be able to handle the powers I can teach her."

He could hardly wait until the next day to begin working with her.

"Ella, your field of study will be conservation and ecology. On these subjects you must gain such an amount of knowledge that you will be a prophet with limitless wisdom. You and I are going to make this planet into a magnificent garden. You will be the reservoir for facts and wise decisions, and I will be the power that turns them into practical reality."

"How could a nut like this be in such a successful position?" Ella asked herself. "Yet," she thought, "his reputation for great achievements is unchallenged. He surely isn't as far out of it all as he seems. My curiosity would drive me crazy if I walked out now."

In the weeks that followed she wondered how she could have been so crazy as to agree to stay. Never before had she worked so hard. She became ensnared in a web of contagious enthusiasm and worked as if under a spell as she directed her life toward a single purpose. The beautiful summer days passed un noticed as she studied inside the windowless walls of the library, and the balmy nights filled with laughing, chattering students slipped by as she continuously buried herself among the ancient stacks of books in the basement. Month after month she studied. environmental problems, natural resource data, and social needs. Ella was always reading and memorizing, but John Sperus was never satisfied.

Finally she decided it was time for a show down. Her worst fears were the suspicion that she had been wasting her time and the whole job was a dead end trip.

"John," she said, "I've been studying and working on all this and there's no end in sight. I don't even know what my objectives are. I feel like the ancient mariner, wondering if I'll ever see land."

It was then that he gave her a series of written and oral tests--a collection of the most comprehensive examinations selected from those devised by top professors at various universities around the nation. To his amazement and delight he found that not only had she packed her brilliant mind with knowledge, but she had gained so much poise and confidence that she could rattle off a rapid fire explanation in answer to any question on ecology or environment.

"Ella," John said eagerly, "you are now a pyramid of knowledge--my rock to built on. I should rename you after some goddess. The new heaven is just around the corner."

"Pardon my skepticism," Ella finally blurted out. "It takes more than knowing about something to bring about change. Many politicians have ended up on the scrap heap of history because they couldn't get their brilliant pieces of legislation through their legislatures. It takes many people working together to build a simple building. The secret of success in human society is the ability to get people to work together."

"Not so, my dear Ella," John exclaimed, jumping up. "Not any more! There is another way. But first, before I divulge the secret, you must be sworn to absolute secrecy. Nothing must ever be said of what I am going to tell you."

"You certainly have my word on that! Silence will be my way of life," Ella agreed, her excitement mounting at the prospect of learning what was really going on.

"Here, at last, is the great secret," John began slowly. "I've never told anyone of this before. You see--I have the power. Yes, THE POWER! I have discovered that anything I believe, so shall it be! If I am convinced that a thing is a certain way, or should be a certain way, or will be a certain way--then that is the way it suddenly becomes. Do you grasp that? I can make anything anyway by truly believing that is how it is! It is an awesome power and I must be sure it is used only for good. The prospect of an error in judgment torments me. So you now must see how you fit into the picture. My power must not be wasted when so many things need to be done; yet, I cannot know everything necessary to make the right decisions. You are now the world's expert on ecology and environment."

"I'm to keep you informed," Ella said, nodding her understanding.

"More than that, you must convince me; for I must believe a thing before it will be that way."

"He's flipped, I think," Ella said to herself. She felt a sinking feeling thinking about her months of study and sacrifice. "But I'm in this thing so deep I'll just have to play along and see what happens."

"Do you see what a responsibility this is?" John continued. "I shudder at what I might create. That is why I must be careful not to drink anything or do something that would cause me to lose conscious control of my every thought. However, you have brought new hope--hope that I can begin to use my power on a broad scale. You will be my balance spring. Do you know there were times when my fear almost drove me to suicide."

"Are you sure about all this? Pardon my saying it, but I'm not sure I really believe things are this way," Ella said apprehensively.

"Well fortunately it is not what you believe, but what I do that is important," John reminded her. "Oh, I can prove what I say, and I expected such a reaction from you. Knowing this day would come, I have long planned a little demonstration for you. With it we can today begin our transformation of the world. At the edge of town there is a small valley I've been watching. It has been heavily damaged by strip mining. The abandoned area is now badly eroded. We will make it into a lush park! Come with me, Ella, and you will soon be convinced."

The dirt road was long abandoned and overgrown with weeds. It wound down along a desolate hillside between rocky cliffs and emerged among devastated knolls and ridges.

Ella felt uneasy as she looked at John. He had a look of elation in his eyes. The zeal of a fanatic radiated from his flushed face.

"What if he goes bananas down here?" she thought. "Some of the most brilliant minds have been known to slip a gear once in a while."

More than a little apprehension crept up her back, when at last the torturing ride with its bumping and swaying, creaking and groaning, came to a halt.

"This is it!" John exclaimed. "Now watch what happens as I believe this will become a beautiful park."

"Wait John," Ella said, grabbing his arm. "There's a little girl hiking over there on the path. What will happen to her?"

"She'll be amazed! That's what will happen to her. She'll find herself in a garden. It will be fun to see her reaction."

"But she'll tell everyone. It will create talk--the suddenness of it all. Maybe we can perform the experiment another time," Ella said, still trying to put off the test and gain time to think.

"Who will take her seriously? She is just a child. Now watch!"

John closed his eyes to concentrate, and then exclaimed, "Isn't it beautiful!"

Ella's face was toward him, watching cautiously, when out of the corner of her eye she detected some movement. Turning her head, she had to blink and pinch herself. For the brown lifeless valley had indeed burst forth into an emerald wonder land. Tall grasses grew beside a gurgling brook and masses of spring flowers turned the hillsides into an artist's palette of color. Blue Jays, Robbins and other birds fluttered among the leafy branches of giant Elm and Sycamore trees.

"Fantastic!" she shouted.

"You see," John smiled. "And see the little girl? She's picking flowers and skipping through the grass."

"Yes, and she's coming this way. Maybe we should leave."

"No, no! Let's talk with her and hear what she says," John insisted.

"See my secret garden?" the little girl shouted. "See! It's just what I've always wanted."

"Sometimes," John said, "if you really wish for something hard enough and have faith, you will get your wish."

"Oh, I really wanted a garden," the girl said. "Only I wish I had a little kitten to play here with me. Do you think if I wish real hard one will come?"

"You can try it," Ella smiled.

"Meew, meew," a tiny voice arose from a white fluffy ball that pounced out of the tall grass.

Two large innocent eyes stared up at them as the little girl squealed with delight.

"That was a nice thing to do, John," Ella nodded.

John looked puzzled.

"Maybe I did it unconsciously. I'm not sure whether I was thinking it or not. That's what scares me!"

"The kitty needs a playmate too," the little girl said.

From out of the tall grass a black and white puff of fur dropped on the first kitten's tail.

"Oh what fun," the little girl screamed.

"Surely I didn't do that!" John said, alarmed. "They must have already been in the valley. I really don't think I did that."

"Maybe we better get out of here," Ella suggested.

"No! Wait! Good Lord! I think she's acquired the power. I think it may have something to do with her being here when I transformed the valley."

"I wish I had a candy playhouse," the little girl shouted.

Her squeal of delight told John and Ella what had happened.

"She has the gift!" John exclaimed with bewilderment.

"Do you really believe that?" Ella asked.

"Yes, of course--can't you see what she's doing. Of course she has the power."

"But John--if anything you believe comes true and you believe she has the power, then you've given it to her. It wasn't until the second kitten appeared that you said you thought she had acquired the gift. You gave it to her then. The kittens probably had nothing to do with it. Remember I was in the valley too."

"Great Scot!"

"To take it away you must believe she doesn't have it," Ella shouted in panic.

"How can I believe that? You can see that she does! "I want to stay here forever," the little girl exclaimed joyfully. I want all the grown-ups to disappear. I want everything to disappear, but my secret garden, my kittens, and me!"

Dramatic Departure

He was willing to leave it all, the bubble house suspended among the trees where the mountains turned pink with the sunrise and the ocean caught fire every evening, his genetically improved dog that could read and converse better than most people, and even his life long friends and the great party they held every Century Eve in the ice caverns of the polar region.

Gazing solemnly toward the green branches, now partly obscured by the ghostly dances of the swirling mists, Ra Isaar, Ecological Consultant for the fourth district, knew the time had come when the past must fall astern in the wake of his life. He could no longer idle away his years in suspended animation.

Although his life was shielded from everything unpleasant so that he felt no pain, desired nothing and had no need that was not instantly fulfilled, he felt a strange restlessness.

"How many centuries have passed since I really felt challenged? How long has it been since my instincts and senses have been keenly alert at the sharpest edge of awareness? When did I last thrill at something new, or gaze with wide eyed wonder and know the feeling of being instantly alive?"

As he asked these questions he felt a surge of determination.

"It has to change!" He clenched his fist in a gesture so rarely used these days. "There has to be more to living This can't be the end product of a long evolution. Is this life, or is this death?"

Ra Isaar's mind pondered the great wonders that had been accomplished. For almost everyone a long life was the rule, and no one aged much as the years passed. Artificial organs and genetic duplicates took care of emergency needs. It seemed that every ancient earthly dream had become a reality.

"Reality!" he shook his head. "What is reality? Do we have the ability to define it anymore? Are the emigrants who go to the other planets, facing unknown hardships, more fortunate than we who stay behind to live in comfort? Would it be insane for me to consider joining that eternal migration?

"Is it madness to even think of subjecting myself to suffering and danger? I could never gain more than I have right here. What is this demon that is driving me?"

He dropped his head, closing his eyes.

"Yet, the only alternative is to continue this nirvana. I fear this is a living death!"

When Ra Isaar visited the office of Eternal Migration he became more confused than ever.

"Of course you know why this office of Eternal Migration was established. You're an executive. I don't have to explain reasons to you."

The man speaking wore the government uniform of the higher echelon and sat behind a polished desk in a bubble room--appropriately enough, high in the clouds.

"But doctor, aren't there less distant trips? Surely we have some ships that aren't for colonial purposes. I was thinking of a ten year space voyage or something like that."

"Most of those are science probes. You'd have to check with Rocket Central about that. Even a ten year trip would be a risk. What of your wife? Have you thought of the consequences for your family?"

"Doctor," Ra Isaar smiled, "we celebrated our two hundred thirty-eighth wedding anniversary five years ago and haven't planned another one until our two hundred fiftieth. She has taken a job with planetary communications on the number two satellite."

"She tired of staying home too I see."

"What is there to do? Everything is automatic. She tuned into all the new book releases every morning and you know how much repetition there is--nothing new or creative. We both studied in ancient, contemporary and future knowledge classes. She even did creative art works and crafts, both ancient and modern forms. Together we studied ESP and brain wave reception until associating with other people was no longer interesting to us."

"Well, you stayed together longer than most," the doctor admitted. "Physical attraction has little retaining power when everyone is young and beautiful."

"And alike!" Ra Isaar added.

"I don't know what else to tell you," the physician said, looking at his watch. "My advice is to take the pills."

"Yes, this is Rocket Central," the voice on the phone answered. "I'll connect you with schedules."

A sympathetic ear, a robot, or a computer was on the other end of the line. From the response to Ra Isaar's request for information it was impossible to tell which.

"As an executive, you should know how swamped we are. We have mounting illegal birth cases and political unstables, not to mention criminals all on holding lists for Eternal Migration. Surely you are a responsible citizen and understand the problems. You would be completely out of place with these passengers, and who knows for sure where the final destinations will be. There is certainly little chance of returning home for centuries, if ever."

"All this I know," Ra Isaar insisted. "I also know there are trips available for more sophisticated, privileged groups, ten year cruises to our affluent colonies, and also voyages for specially selected groups to carry our culture throughout the universe. These voyages are completely unpublicized."

The existence of such trips was often rumored, and Ra's bluff brought out the truth.

"These are available only on the recommendation of a physician. The waiting lists are long and the trips are very expensive. See your physician."

"I've already seen my physician."

"And he said."

"He gave me some pills."

"The problem is concluded. A sensible solution."

At four in the morning the automatic timer clicked and a large plastic sign illuminated the vacant square. The innocent looking black letters ETERNAL MIGRATION looked down on the locked iron gate below. The courtyard, enclosed by a solid wall of dark brick buildings with black, sightless windows, was deserted.

Suddenly a dark shadow formed a salient, advancing across the paving. The first customer had arrived. He was a richly dressed, prosperous looking man wearing a blue cape trimmed with gold fir and he was carrying a matching blue and gold bag.

Stopping for a moment, he glanced around the deserted square and then, without further hesitancy walked toward the Eternal Migration gate. He was about twenty-five yards from his destination when he froze and remained as still as a statue with one foot up in the air.

It was then that a second shadow shot from a darkened doorway and a man emerged, running, tucking a paralysis gun into his belt. As he reached the petrified traveler he quickly removed the man's tickets and identification. When he pulled off the blue cape he attached something to the man's back and spoke softly to his stunned victim.

"I know you can hear me, although you can't move. Listen carefully. I have placed a lift pack on your back and set it for one hundred feet. That will put you up in the clouds. The paralysis will wear off in two hours at which time you can safely return to the ground by pulling the cord on your shoulder. No doubt your physician can get you another ticket for a voyage at some future time."

Like a monkey on a string, one leg still in the air, the rigid figure rose into the haze above. Below him on the courtyard several large buses arrived. These bud shaped vehicles opened like flowers and the passengers swarmed out, covering the pavement like ants. In the midst of the confusion it was easy for Ra Isaar, with his new identity and ticket, to flow through the open gate along with the excited group.

He felt like he was dreaming, drawn by a great magnate along moving stairways, floated up escalators, and sucked into the hissing space projectile.

"Free!" Ra smiled to himself. "At last freedom from the living death. A new world to conquer. I, Ra Isaar, the emigrant."

The lift off was fast and painless--almost too uneventful for such a momentous time. The planet was dropping rapidly behind when the soft music from the intercom was interrupted by the mellow, automatic voice of the flight instructor.

"Welcome aboard flight two ninety-three for Albion II. As class A emigrants you will find nothing has been overlooked to provide for your comfort. We will arrive at our destination at 0300 exactly three years from today. The weather on Albion II will be clear and sunny on that day. Rain gear will not be needed when you leave the ship.'

"Your rocket is a Century Alpha luxury cruiser and this model has a one hundred percent safety record in over four hundred flights. However, in case of emergency please observe the following instructions. When the computer indicates a rocket disaster is inevitable, your bubble stateroom will be automatically ejected into space and a message will be sent out instructing rescue rockets of your location.

"Should the computer be damaged and unable to do the ejecting, you have a manual control, a red lever, next to your bed. This will do the same job and relay automatic SOS messages. Your bubble is self contained and you can live for seven years awaiting rescue. Should rescue never come, or should you become terminally ill or be in great pain, there is a red bottle of vaporizing pills in your medicine cabinet.

"So much for that! And now back to the pleasant, since we feel sure you will never need to use emergency measures. Your stateroom has crystal walls, behind which have been projected green trees and scenic landscapes. These have been designed by Art Central professionals. You will probably think you never left home.

"At your finger tips are a wide variety of cine-vision favorites, a great collection of tapes of your favorite music, and every morning you will receive all the new book releases relayed from Earth.

"Contemporary and future knowledge classes will be held in the lounge daily, and creative art works and crafts will be in the recreation room each afternoon. For food, the selectomatic in your stateroom can bring you any desired delicacy at the touch of a finger.

"It will be years of travel, but you can rest assured everything possible has been done to make this environment exactly like the one to which you are accustomed. Many of our class A emigrants have expressed surprise at such speedy arrivals, saying they had forgotten they had left home.

Another voice, soft and feminine, added more honey and syrup.

"The biggest surprise will be Albion II. It is a pleasant planet, selected because of almost identical climate and similar features to Earth. Many new cities have been built and you will find you have left no conveniences behind.

"Now, please go to your staterooms if you have not already done so. You can communicate on the talk screen. If you need anything our staff of robots will efficiently serve you."

As Ra entered his room, number one hundred ninety-three, he was stunned! He blinked, shook his head and rubbed his eyes.

"I must be dreaming after all. I must wake ups"

The crystal walls of the room glowed with pink mountains and green trees as the sound circle overhead blew out the soft sounds of his favorite music.

He reached out and touched the solid wall and fell back upon the cloud-like bed.

My opium existence has followed me! My life is still inside a cocoon!"

Closing his eyes, he felt more trapped than ever.

"Is anything real?" he asked himself.

As he once more opened his eyes and looked around, he saw swirling mists among the green branches, but he also saw some vibrant red next to his bed. Reaching out, he felt his hand touch cold steel. The solid metal was made for his grip, and as he clenched his fingers around it, it sent a chill up his back.

"This is real, and this is new!" he exclaimed, Grinding his teeth with determination, Ra pulled the lever with all his strength.

He felt a sudden acceleration and an invisible hand forced him against the wall.

"Emergency 193! Emergency 193!" shouted the voice on the screen. "Answer 193!"

Ra Isaar stared in dazed silence at the excited face.

"Come in 193. Are you injured? Answer 193!"

As the fingers of force holding him against the wall relaxed, Ra walked over to the voice screen, and with calm deliberation grasped the connecting wires and jerked them out.

On the walls the pink mountains continued to glow and the swirling mists continued to dance among the trees. Across the room, on the opposite wall, an ocean blazed with a golden sunset. From overhead the ethereal music was blowing softly into his ears. And below--what was that below? Something was flickering.

Sparks? Hot wires? No! Not fire! Stars!

Ra rushed to the glowing place on the floor.

"The opaque paint is gone. The surface must have been scraped during ejection! I have a window! A view window on the universe!"

The window was studded with glowing coals. Far astern he could see Earth, a blue sapphire planet. Off toward the Milky Way there was a ghostly comet with a flowing veil speeding toward the mysterious caverns of space.

Already the Century Alpha rocket had disappeared. No doubt rescue rockets would be quickly dispatched from Earth, but the bubble was tiny and might be difficult to find. However, Ra knew that with precise efficiency the searchers would eventually find him, even if he succeeded in jamming the little radio that was sending out SOS signals.

In the meantime Ra Isaar would sit on the floor of this glass bottom boat as it hurtled through space and he would drink in the eternal glory of the timeless universe. He would lie on his stomach with his nose pressed against the glass, marveling at each new discovery and feeding his imagination with endless fantasies. There would be planets, stars, comets, nebulae, asteroids, distant galaxies and so many more cosmic wonders!

Of course those Earth patrols with their rescue squads would find him. They always found lost space travelers. They never gave up even if it took years. They had a record, a reputation to maintain. They'd find him for sure! They'd find him, but it might take a long time. When they did, it would be time for the red bottle in the medicine cabinet.

Moon's Children

"I knew it would happen," Marie said shaking her head. "It was predictable. It's the way the young people were raised! I could tell by the things the kids said, the questions they asked, their discussions and comments. I knew it!"

"Well it all took me by surprise I guess. It surprised me and depressed me. I really thought things had changed more than that. I thought our greater emphasis on education and all the money spent on research had really changed things. Good Lord, Marie, I'm disillusioned."

"I guess we all feel a little that way Mark--at least we who are immigrants."

"I really feel lost and alone," Mark said, "more like an alien than ever. Where do we go from here, Marie?"

"We just try to adjust, unless you want to go back; but I know the kids would never leave. They are enthusiastic about everything that's happened. The generation gap has become a chasm. We don't know them anymore and they don't know us."

"I feel it too and wonder. Where did it all begin? Where did we go astray in our training and education? For surely we all have to share in the blame for bringing about these dramatic changes. Changes we don't want, but they do. Personally I feel they are out to make all the mistakes of the past all over again. It's ancient history repeating itself."

"Mark, I think it came about so gradually we didn't recognize the minute daily changes. It's like when one grows old we don't notice it day by day. Then one day we look in a mirror and the reality smacks us in the face.

"We were all so busy pursuing daily objectives that we didn't notice our course was a degree or two off. As we traveled on, that tiny degree eventually caused a deviation in our path so great that our desired course was no longer in view, or attainable. The chances for a course correction that would make things as we once visualized them are now gone forever."

"I guess we blew it all when we ignored the tiny danger signals," Mark agreed.

"That is so true. I used to marvel at the children's questions and their sophistication, yet naiveness, about things. I remember that conversation with Anna when she was young. She wanted to know about weather. I remember when she came into the library with that puzzled look on her face. Electrus had just fixed the thermostat and he had used the word 'weather.'"

"What is weather?" Anna asked. "Did he say the earth has weather?"

"Yes, dear," I explained to her, "weather is when the air and sky change. Sometimes the sky grows dark even during the day, and it may rain."

"Black?" Anna asked. "You mean like at night when we can't see the sun for two weeks and the craters are all dark except for the earthlight?"

"No, honey, not black like night. It is more gray. Large clouds form in the sky and you can't see the sun or the stars."

"Clouds?"

"Yes. You've seen the plastic dome over the main crater get foggy so you can't see up through it. Clouds are sort of like that, only they are great masses of water vapor that are floating above. They look like smoke."

"Oh, now I remember," Anna nodded. "Electrus says those are the things that cause water to fall--uh--rain. He said it's like the water dripping from the domes when it's cold outside."

"Rain is something like that," I explained to her. "Only it comes down hard. Sometimes it feels a little like someone is throwing sand in your face."

"Oh, I wouldn't like that."

"No, you probably wouldn't," I said. "Sometimes so much rain falls that it forms great pools of water and it even washes land away. And it flows in great rivers to the sea."

"I've seen pictures of the sea. Where could so much water come from? It makes most of the earth useless. My teacher said that is why everything is so crowded there. We can use all of the surface of the moon. Moon is all beautiful mountains and rocks. And the moon doesn't keep changing. In Lunology Dr. Croctus said that on the earth everything keeps getting worn down and washed away."

"That is called erosion. The wind and the rain wear down mountains, make sand dunes and do all kinds of things."

"I don't think I could get used to wind. Dr. Croctus says it's all over the earth and it's invisible. It tears up things and knocks things down without warning."

"When the wind blows it can do damage, but it doesn't usually hurt anything."

"I like the air the way we have it."

"Yes, here all the elements are controlled. The air machines keep the craters filled to the domes and everything is kept at a comfortable temperature."

"And the air doesn't rush around!"

"No, you never hear the wind noises--never hear it rustling the leaves of the trees."

"We have a tree in the east crater, next to the zoo. It's scary! I don't like trees! They are so big, and twisted and creepy. Electrus says they are really alive!"

"Yes, dear. The earth is covered with them."

"Aach! Water and air rushing around and big old trees and plants everywhere! Earth is an awful, scary place!"

"But children on the earth like to climb the trees and swim in the water. And on a cool summer evening it's nice to smell the scent of the flowers. I remember how fresh everything was after a rain. And even snow, frozen rain, was nice. It settled on the ground and we could play in it and slide down the hills on it."

"Mom, sometimes you're weird. All that messy stuff!"

"And it was relaxing to see the ocean waves breaking on the rocks, to watch birds gliding over the sea, and to see sunsets on the water when the clouds were like fire."

"You have more nerve than I have. I wouldn't sit by a lot of unstable water with living things flying around my head, and all the time the sky looking like a big explosion. I'd bury my head in the sand. Dr. Croctus says the earth gets dark for a few hours and then light for a few hours, then dark for a few hours and then light again. And he said every few months everything changes. He says you wouldn't recognize some places because they change so much. It must really be crazy. I don't see how you could stand to live in a place like that."

Marie looked at her husband's serious face.

"Those were Anna's own words, Mark. She didn't see how I could stand living in a jungle like the earth. You see we should have recognized what was happening to our children then."

"Yes, I've had similar conversations with the children also. Johnny couldn't understand why anyone would stay on the earth, and when I suggested a vacation there he was horrified. There were bacteria and virus contaminations all over. The very thought of insects is too much for him. A bug of any kind sends him into a state of shock. In fact, when he was in college he even suggested the whole planet be condemned as a health hazard. He wanted the earth to be off limits to Moonites!

"There is no doubt about our letting our children drift away from their heritage, but many of the changes I feel are economic. Since Moon has become self sufficient in minerals and technology, and her people have mastered the art of lunar food production, the Moonites have developed a superiority complex. A lot of the top brains and affluent people came to the moon to escape the earth's problems, and now they want to sever the umbilical cord. They want to slam the door on future growth. Neither do they want the problems to follow them, nor do they want to share their new found haven with others. You have to admit this is a comfortable existence with a perfect climate and an answer to every need at the finger tips."

"I don't know, Mark," Marie said, "I still feel like an alien. I guess it is a feeling of guilt, or my sense of responsibility to the people of Earth."

"I think we've been passed up by history, old girl! It's not a dream. It has happened. Moon has revolted and won her independence. The new world has broken with the old!"

Julie's World

The night sky seemed darker than usual to Aldena as she slowly, cautiously slipped among the shrubbery, dashing from shadow to shadow, working her way along the edge of the driveway that led to the house. The concrete walk was gray under the starlight and reached out toward her like an elephant's trunk trying to pull her to the old building.

Aldena felt a sinking feeling as she looked at the dark windows and listened to the absolute silence around her. She knew she could turn back and flee to the lighted street, but if she didn't keep going she would hate herself in the morning when bright sunlight dissolved the fears of the night.

"Keep calm, Aldena," she said to herself. "Don't let your emotions run away!"

By forcing herself to put one foot in front of the other, she crossed the open walk, climbed the six broad steps and stood on the dingy flagstone terrace in front of the massive wood door. A large, black, iron lantern hung over the doorway, but there was no light to brighten the porch.

"Surely," she thought, "this place has long been deserted. Can cousin Julie really be living here?"

Yet, Aldena was sure of the address. This had to be, the place her mother had mentioned. Her mind went back over that argument that had led her to this strange predicament.

"I can't believe it Mother! Here I am twenty-one years old and no one ever told me about Julie. I have a cousin living just a mile and a half away and no one ever mentioned her. If it hadn't been for Margaret Cole I don't suppose I ever would have known."

"She had no business talking about the confidential records she handles," Mrs. Davis had answered angrily.

"All she did was to ask me how my cousin Julie was. Imagine! Here I didn't even know I had a cousin. I felt like a fool!"

"Aldena, listen! This is your mother you're talking to," Mrs. Davis interrupted. "You're delving into something that can hurt you as well as Julie. Do you think we have some sinister reason for not telling you about Julie? Do you think your relatives are all insensitive fools? Does the record indicate we haven't been interested in your welfare in everything we've done? Be sensible! Believe me there are good reasons we haven't told you about Julie. It is most important that you leave this matter alone."

"Is she handicapped in some way? Are Julie's looks a disgrace to the family?" Aldena asked angrily.

"No, no Aldena, you're on the wrong track. She's a beautiful girl. As a baby she was like an angel doll."

"Then it's mental! That's why the family is ashamed of her, isn't it? I've heard of skeletons in the closet, but I never thought my own family......"

"No one is ashamed of Julie!" Mrs. Davis shouted angrily. "What has been done is best for Julie. I'm not going to quarrel with you. Forget Julie. You are not going to see her!"

The conversation had ended abruptly with a challenge that Aldena could not let pass, so she now found herself standing in front of this great stone building with its massive shadows that were hovering about her like a cloak, threatening to engulf her.

"Surely Julie could not live here," she said to herself. "There isn't any light, and I haven't heard a sound! The place is deserted!"

Timidly she reached out and touched the cold brass of the door latch. To her surprise and shock the door easily swung open revealing a dark, cave-like entry hall. After hesitating for a minute to muster some courage, Aldena forced her feet to inch forward slowly until she was inside.

It took several minutes for her eyes to adjust to the absence of light and her imagination filled the darkness with phantoms before the real objects began to take shape.

The outline of a chair appeared, followed by the gnarled fingers of a hat and coat stand. A huge chandelier hung high above a curved stairway that led up to an even darker cavern.

As she strained her eyes, she could see that it was not all dark on the second floor. A whisper of light, like a bit of mist, lay on the floor, oozing out from under a door. It was toward this beacon, like a ship at sea on a stormy night, that Aldena hastened.

The suffocating silence made a knock on the door out of the question. Surely a sudden noise would shatter everything--the darkness, and even the house. Quietly she opened the door and was overcome with a flood of light that rushed out and stung her eyes.

In the room there was an old table with a half empty bottle of wine on it, and beside the table, sitting in an old wooden rocking chair, was a stout, middle aged woman. The woman's head was bent forward and she was snoring softly. In her hand, resting on the white apron in her lap, was an empty glass.

Startled to have come upon a person, Aldena quickly closed the door. She felt ashamed of her aggressive action in walking into someone's room without knocking. She realized she was an intruder who had invaded someone's privacy and she hurried back to the head of the stairs.

However, as she started down the stairs she stopped again. There was another sound, very faint and far away, tugging at her ears. Soft music was tumbling down the stairs from some upstairs room.

As she hesitated and strained, to see better, the darkness suddenly exploded like a photographer's flash. Bright lights from the massive chandelier chased every shadow from the room. There was no place to hide. She was exposed--naked in the spotlight.

Almost immediately a flame of golden red flashed on the landing above, and then swept down the stairs. Thank God! It was a living girl--with a radiant smile and sunlit hair.

"I knew you were here!" the girl cried out to her. "You did come to the party didn't you?"

"You startled me," Aldena choked.

"Well, why didn't you turn on the lights? You'd never find the ball room in the dark. Come on Aldena, I'll show you the way."

"You know my name?" Aldena asked with surprise. "Who are you?"

"Julie. Your cousin Julie. Come on. The others will miss me."

Julie grabbed Aldena's hand and led her back up the stairs and down the hall.

"I don't understand this," Aldena said. "I only found out about you yesterday. I didn't even know I had a cousin." Her voice sounded far away as it echoed through the house. Suddenly everything seemed unreal.

"Oh, I've only known about you for a little while too," Julie said. "Of course I've been dying to meet you ever since Dr. Arvis said you were coming over. He's the one who heard you downstairs."

The lights and the music grew more intense as they neared a half open door.

"I don't remember a Dr. Arvis," Aldena said, frowning, "and I didn't know I was coming here myself until tonight. I'm sure I didn't tell anyone."

"Well," Julie smiled, "I'm so glad you're here at last. I'm sorry it's so crowded. I really would like to have a long talk with you alone."

Leaning toward her, Julie cupped her mouth with one hand, "Maybe they'll leave soon."

Aldena looked around the large room. There was a double bed in the corner, a small fireplace, two upholstered chairs along the wall, a desk with a lamp on it by the window, a small table with a record player next to the bed, and a full length mirror by the wardrobe door--a mirror that reflected just two people, Julie and herself. Nowhere in the room was anyone else to be seen.

"I think your guests have slipped away already," she whispered to Julie.

"If it were only true! Come on, I'll introduce you," Julie said, grabbing her by the arm.

"It's a party for Uncle Albert," she explained. "Aldena, this is Diane--and of course Jerry."

She covered her mouth again, "They're always together. She can't get away from him for a minute.

"And this is Mr. Jenkens," she continued in a louder voice. "Mr. Jenkens, my cousin Aldena. Oh, and Dr. Arvis. You were right again Doctor. Here she is! My cousin, Aldena.

"Now let's see. You'll never remember all these names, if you're like me. Over by the window is Betty James and her husband Carl, and that older woman is Janet Everet.

"I do wish you had gotten here earlier. Grandma Swanson was here. She always wants to go to bed early. But then I guess you see her all the time yourself. She and your grand father love to play gin rummy."

"Julie, I can't stay long," Aldena interrupted. "I just wanted to stop in and say hello. Now that I know where you live I'll come back again soon. You know--when we can talk alone."

"You can't run off now! You just got here, and the party is just starting," Julie held her arm tightly.

"But I must," Aldena insisted.

"I'll not hear of it for a minute. And see. They all want you to stay too."

"I really must. Goodnight everybody. Glad to have met you all," Aldena said, backing toward the door.

"Well, alright," Julie pouted, "but promise you'll come again tomorrow."

"I'll try," Aldena promised, as she backed into the hall.

"Shall I show you to the door?" Julie asked.

"No, you stay with your guests. I can find my way," Aldena said, waving and smiling.

"Thank you for coming," Julie said, and she waved back.

As Aldena went out the front door she glanced back and could still see that little flame at the top of the stairs. How good the crisp night air felt on her face as she hurried home.

"What are you doing up so early?" Mrs. Davis asked with surprise. "I didn't expect you would be having breakfast with me at this hour during your vacation. When you wrote home from college you said you were going to sleep until noon every day during your break."

"I couldn't sleep much last night, thinking of Julie. I went to see her," Aldena confessed.

"I thought you would," her mother nodded grimly. "Are you satisfied now?"

"It was frightening last night, but this morning I realize how stupid the whole thing is. Julie needs to see a doctor--a psychiatrist. She may even have a chemical imbalance."

"Don't you think we've thought of that? She has been examined repeatedly, and treated."

"Well, she certainly won't get well being treated as she is! That's probably what a lot of the trouble is. She's being kept in a world apart. When I was there last night that whole great estate seemed to float in a bubble of nothingness. I felt as if I had been sucked into a capsule and surrounded by a vacuum. The feeling was eerie. The place is an enclave, a balloon drifting on the surface of the earth, but not part of it."

"It isn't the place, Aldena," her mother said. "That is the way everyone feels around Julie...no matter where Julie is."

"There was a woman in the house. When I peeked into a room I saw her dozing in a chair. She had been drinking wine I think. Who is she? Not my aunt, Julie's mother, is she? Do I have a living aunt and uncle I don't know about also?"

"That was the house keeper. Your Aunt Martha and Uncle William never stay there anymore. They travel most of the time."

"So they are Julie's parents! I thought they didn't have any children. We seem to only hear from them when we get a card at Christmas. Aren't they the ones you were telling me about--the ones who don't get along together very well?"

"They certainly don't," her mother nodded. "That is, they haven't gotten along well since Julie was a baby."

"It sounds as if they are messing up their own lives and Julie's too," Aldena snapped.

"Maybe it's the other way around," Mrs. Davis said defensively. "Certainly Julie was at the center of the controversy. If Uncle William hadn't been color blind the shock wouldn't have been so great. He wouldn't have made such a fool of himself.

"You know how some men are color blind. They are born without the receptors in the back of their eyes, those cones and rods that detect certain colors. When a man is color blind for red, he just doesn't see that color. It can be all around him and he can be looking right at it, but for him it just doesn't exist. That was the way with Uncle William. He was color blind for red, and Julie has bright red hair. But why go into all this now. It's all water under the bridge."

"Go on, Mother, I've got to know," Aldena insisted.

Mrs. Davis looked at her daughter's face and she knew she would never give up. She never did. Where did she get that persistence? Neither her father nor mother were so unrelenting. Children were not always like their parents. That was what Uncle William didn't realize.

"When Julie was born," Mrs. Davis continued, "Uncle William and Aunt Martha were very happy. He went around giving out the usual cigars and joyfully received everyone's congratulations. Julie was as beautiful a child as you will ever see. People called her an angel doll because she was radiant.

"It was after the christening that everything changed. There was a party and a lot of people had a little too much to drink, with the spiked punch and a few bottles on the side. Someone made a crack like, 'She's a pretty little doll, but who are her parents?' and this was followed by someone asking, 'Where did she get the red hair?'

"Uncle William and Aunt Martha both had black hair. No one realized that Uncle William was color blind and that he didn't know that Julie's hair was red."

"I thought that color blind people could still see some differences," Aldena said.

"Each case is different, depending on what receptors are missing from the eyes. Your Uncle William had no color receptors at all. He could look at a rainbow and never even see it. If everyone were like that, we wouldn't even know there was such a thing as color. We probably wouldn't even have words for blue, green, yellow or red."

"It might have its blessings," Aldena said. "It would help to solve a major human problem."

"When your Uncle William found out about Julie's red hair he became so upset, that after the guests had gone he accused Aunt Martha of being unfaithful. Of course he'd been drinking. He demanded to know who the father was, and said no one in his family had ever had red hair. He wanted to know if Aunt Martha could name anyone in her family that had ever had red hair.

"Aunt Martha was shocked. She couldn't remember anyone in her family with red hair, but tried to explain the complications of genetics. But it was all very hopeless."

"How stupid!" Aldena shouted in disbelief. "How could Uncle William be so dumb?"

"Uncle William scoffed at Aunt Martha's explanations and ridiculed her, insisting she had been unfaithful. He refused to acknowledge Julie as his child.

"Poor Julie. There was no love in that house. Martha tried to take care of the baby herself, but when Julie started acting so strange it became too much for her. She became frightened and exhausted and eventually had a complete nervous break down. That was when they hired a housekeeper to take care of Julie.

"Martha was so distraught that one time she said she was sure the babies were switched at the hospital. Another time she said the devil was Julie's father. At any rate, she and Uncle William seemed to write Julie out of their lives and they took to traveling.

"How terrible!" Aldena exclaimed, "Such medieval, superstitious relatives I have. The problem isn't Julie's at all. It's her parents."

"Well, it was wrong of them, but it isn't easy. Julie is a strange one."

"You mean because she imagines things? No wonder she does. She's so lonely, and has been all of her life. She makes up people just to satisfy her longing. Who wouldn't?"

"It isn't that simple, Aldena. She's always been that way. When she was a tiny girl she was always frightened. She would cry and scream, 'Mother, make them go away. Make those people go away.' Her mother could never convince her there was no one else there. She would take her by the hand and lead her around the room telling her to look everywhere and pointing out there was no one else there, but it was useless. Julie would just scream, 'Make them go away! Make them all go away!' No one could reason with her. It was always the same."

"Is that all?" Aldena snorted. "A little child frightened by her own imagination? Older people in rest homes get the same way, but no one shuts them away somewhere. It would be cruel."

"No one tried to shut her away. They even tried sending her to school, but the more people that were around her the worse she got. She would go up to the other children and ask them who all their friends were when they were alone. She was always talking and playing games with imaginary people. It became impossible. Other children ridiculed her and she became miserable.

"You know what I think," Aldena interrupted again, "I think her whole condition is because of Aunt Martha and Uncle William rejecting her. This is a perfect example of causing a person to be a problem and then justifying your treatment of her. How would you like some one refusing to accept you as you are, deciding how you should live, and then forcing you to live that way?"

"With Julie's case it isn't that way," Mrs. Davis insisted. "She was scared and miserable, but in her own world she is happy."

"I think she should be examined by a doctor," Aldena said.

"That's what we all said. She was sent to the best clinics in the country. Even at the clinics she kept seeing imaginary people and talking with them all around the doctors.

"No one really figured out Julie's problem, but Dr. Arvis discovered a physical condition he wanted to investigate further. The whole thing was dropped when he and his assistant, Mr. Jenkens were killed in an auto accident.

"It seems she has some different kinds of cones and rods in the back of her eyes--receptors unlike any ever seen in a human eye before.

"Your Uncle Albert was doing research and planned to write a book about their theories, but he died before he got much done. Your Grandma Swanson had his notes, but I don't know what happened to them after she died.

"If Dr. Arvis and Mr. Jenkens had lived maybe they could have done something for Julie."

"You mean all those people are dead!" Aldena gasped. "They're the ones Julie introduced!"

Always A Chance

"Fellow travelers, you are all in a period of transition. You are here in space on your way to the other world--a world about which you know nothing at all.

"Oh, I'm sure the wise men have preached to you about it and their disciples have taught you how to prepare yourselves for that day of arrival; but I can tell you now they know nothing of what they speak! None have ever been there. They are very idealistic in their approach. They give assurances and cleverly cover their ignorance. However, I am as you say, 'down to earth,' although I can't really say that when we are drifting in the void of space millions of miles from the planet. Let me say instead that I am direct and without rose colored glasses. I am from that other world, and I know it. And I can assure you that it is nothing like you expect!"

The tall man dressed in a conservative dark suit held the attention of everyone in the space ship as he paced back and forth. He spoke with a voice that rose and fell, each undulation emphasizing a particular point. He used his extra long arms and long fingers to create stick like patterns all around him that changed in shape with each inflection in his voice. He was the center of a strobe light, dominating the entire scene with deep, distant blue eyes that had the glow of a welder's torch and the glint of a fanatic--blue eyes that be came as hard as steel or as mellow as music from one moment to the next.

"How can those who have never taken a journey teach you of the hazards and perils?" he went on. "Who really knows of the other world? I don't like to be the bearer of bad tidings, but I cannot let you continue without the knowledge of some basic facts about what awaits you. That is my mission. I've come sweeping out to meet you in this eternal emptiness, to minister to your needs and properly prepare you for the coming days.

"My two companions and I have braved the many perils in our tiny ship in order to do our duty and give you guidance. Fellow travelers that is our purpose and our calling.

"I am Artimus Innes, and here beside me now is D. R. Lamm. D. R. Lamm is the expert on the very first problems you will encounter and I plead with you--implore you--to listen intensely, for your own sakes!"

Turning slightly and dropping his voice he addressed the man at his side.

"D.R., here are two hundred twenty-three migrants from Earth traveling to the other world on the Eternus space ship number seventy-two, and you can see by their innocent faces they need much counseling and advising. Enlighten them so they will not proceed blindly. They are as tragically unprepared for the next world as have been all the other Earth immigrants we have encountered."

Again turning to face the passengers, he waved his broom stick arm and pointed it straight at the man beside him, who because of his smaller stature, seemed lost in shadows and hardly noticeable.

Once D.R. Lamm stepped into the limelight, however, it was apparent that although he was short he was a dynamo of personal magnitude. His short cut hair capped a face that was pierced with sharp brown eyes, giving him an alert, ferocious appearance. Thin, pale lips sealed a grim, straight mouth, and if D. R. Lamm ever smiled there was no evidence of it in the lines of his face. However, he proved to be a forceful speaker.

"Until now," he began with a low penetrating voice, "you've had an uneventful trip. Everything has gone like clockwork. So well, in fact, that you've been lulled into a false sense of security.

"You look around. There are the solid, familiar walls of your space craft--strong shields against the external forces around us. The soft lights play upon the colorful surroundings. The dishes are in place. The bed is ready. Soft music soothes the nerves. God's in his heaven--all's right with the world.

"Inside you feel as secure as a babe in his mother's arms. You are warm and comfortable in your cocoon. Yet, how fragile is your world!"

"You are as a person in an airliner flying over a jungle. As long as there is no unknown force and all systems function you can lead your comfortable, modern existence; but let one little thing malfunction, forcing you to land and you are suddenly in a primitive world filled with a million hazards. Survival itself becomes the only preoccupation. Time has been turned back on you and you must adapt to the ancient life of the savage. You were only minutes from your destination with all its comforts and conveniences, when abruptly you were separated from everything for months or even years. In essence you have in a few seconds lost centuries of advancement.

"The things I have outlined are the things you must be come aware of now! Such a tragedy may well await you all!

"Your ship must fly through vast space that is filled with time distortions--bubbles of ancient time are floating around you just waiting to be pierced by your ship. You may be engulfed by who knows what historic place or period! On the other hand you may be snapped as if by a rubber band, right out into some distant universe where even the basic matter is different from our own--one with different size electrons and protons, with larger or smaller molecules throughout. You would be alien matter in every conceivable way.

"And don't forget the black holes in space--those magnetic maelstroms with such power that not even light can escape. You could be drawn to them into eternity and there is no known force to overcome that collapsing gravity.

"These things may never happen to you; but they could! And I regret to tell you there is no protection from these natural disasters.

"For whatever happens, however, I do bring hope; for I represent the Space Archipelago Group. This is a federation of beings from all over the galaxy that maintains a bureau to trace citizens such as you into time, place, or universe and to devise methods of returning them to their proper destinations. To carry out such responsibilities is an awesome task; but the members of our group never give up and our successes are amazing.

"Of course the costs are also great and for that reason we must sell policies in order to continue our good work. And regretfully also, because of the costs we can only take care of our policy holders.

"Think what it would mean to be locked into a hostile place, and think of the hopelessness if no one were working for your release!

"I will pass out applications to you all. If you wish this protection for yourselves and your families, just fill in the blank spaces and answer the questions. Bring the signed copies to me later today and we can conclude our agreements."

"Thank you, D. R.," Artimus Innes stepped forward once more. "I'm sure these people feel much better now, knowing that your group is always ready--anxious, to seek out anyone who is lost and to return that person to safety.

"And now good people," he continued, "I know you are wondering about this silent man to my right."

Again he waved his stick like arm until it finally landed on the shoulders of the very straight, broad shouldered man beside him. As Artimus' fingers curled around the man's arm, the silent one stepped quickly forward as if to escape a closing vice. Oblivious to the man's evasive move, Artimus Innes continued the introduction.

"This is Elman Roose, a man with many years experience in the most distant parts of space. He is a true expert on the other hazards you may encounter."

Although Elman Roose did not have any exceptional features that would make him stand out in a crowd, his face wore the wise look of one who had been through it all and knows all the answers. Through his glasses peered two eyes with the steady look of self confidence. Standing erect, with hands clasped behind him, he began.

"Although the dangers my colleague, D.R. Lamm, has explained to you are certainly real, they are by no means the most serious problems that await you!

"It has been said on Earth that most of man's problems are man made, and philosophers have long decried man's inhumanity to man. The people saying these things are certainly right. There is no escaping the truth of such statements. And there is no escaping such problems by going into space either!

"I'm sure you have learned that there are many other intelligent creatures besides man--superior beings scattered throughout the galaxies of the universe. Many civilizations are far more advanced in culture, science, and......in destructive ability!

"Just as man's progress from ancient times has included the refinements of primitive methods and the development of sophisticated machines to do the same old tasks and fulfill the same old desires--including devices for war and battle, so has it been the same with other intelligent beings. Just as the people of Earth had difficulty overcoming that ancient survival tendency to be suspicious of the environment and hostile toward any beings outside of their own group as a way of protecting their own kind, so have other beings in space had these difficulties! Had all living beings not been suspicious and defensive, they probably would not have been long survivors in this universe."

Leaning closer to the audience, Elman Roose peered so intently that his thick lenses seemed as search lights radiating beams that engulfed first one individual and then another. He reached forward holding out an open palm.

"I tell you all this so you will understand that to most of the universe you are aliens! Outsiders, to be viewed with suspicion, distrust and hostility! The surest way to be safe is to destroy a potential threat before it can harm you. Even if there is doubt about a thing being a threat, destroy it anyhow Why take chances? I think you from Earth understand this logic.

"How does this concern you? This ship is no doubt under surveillance now. You may be spotted and attacked anywhere in space long before you reach your destination.

"What can be done about it? Fortunately, a great deal! Our group constructed, at great cost, a fleet of escort ships armed with weapons so advanced that you've never dreamed of such power. Never have we encountered a hostile ship we could not handle; and it's no wonder, for we were taught by the most ancient civilization in Andromeda. And our reputation has spread so that just the sight of our fleet is enough to discourage any enemy group.

"Of course we cannot sell individual policies for such protection. We could not protect a few without protecting all. Therefore we ask that ninety percent of the passengers agree to pay the premium. Everyone should! But we know that there are always a few free loaders. Our fleet will then escort your ship all the way to the next world. Frankly, if you don't agree to hang together in the common defense, it is my opinion that you are doomed.

"I'll pass out cards. Just sign them and return them to me if you want the defensive escort."

Like a sudden flash of light Artimus Innes again jumped up.

"Thank you Elman, I'm sure these people are intelligent enough to take the necessary precautions and know how to act together. And while they are signing the cards I'll explain another way we can help them.

"There is one other condition all you immigrants to the other world must understand. The laws are different. People are often punished because of their inabilities to explain their actions. In other words you may break a law unknowingly, or you may already have broken one. That may seem a little hard to understand, but things are different where you are going. They are very particular about immigrants. You will be investigated and your mind and memory will be scanned. All of your past actions will be enumerated by the computer.

"This is a phase of immigration that the public employees of Earth never explain to anyone. Maybe they don't know about it, or just believe that such stories are idle rumors.

"At any rate, you may well be called to account for things in your past life, and may even face punishment. However, again my group can help you. We can provide the service necessary to avoid such unpleasantness. We can examine you privately and certify you to be a good citizen. Our guarantee of your good citizenship will be accepted by the authorities. You see we have established a reputation of trust by our excellent record. Ninety-nine percent of the immigrants we have supported have become excellent citizens.

"Of course it is a costly business to have one to one meetings with immigrants. It takes highly trained and highly paid personnel to staff the program. However, I'm sure you will find it worth the necessary fee. The applications will be available from me at your request."

After holding up the papers for everyone to see, Artimus Innes bowed almost to the floor.

"We are all your humble servants who have risked the dangers of space in our small craft in order to further the humanitarian work of our group."

The three speakers then walked to the rear of the compartment and sat down at a small table which became an ant hill of business and confusion as the immigrants surrounded it.

At the other end of the room the ship's captain and a steward leaned against the walls with their coffee mugs in their hands watching the excited immigrants.

"It's always this way," the captain said.

"How many of these flights have you been on?" the steward asked.

"Quite a few," the captain answered, "and this always happens."

"Is it really the way they say it is? Are the dangers really that great?"

"Who really knows about space? Every one of my seven flights has ended this way. Most of the passengers will sign up for everything. We'll have a fleet of escort ships tomorrow and they'll fly along side of us until we land."

"Do you think anything would happen if the people just said 'no' and saved their money?"

"Most people feel they've come so far that they just don't want anything to happen. Why take chances?"

"You've never hit a time bubble or come close to a black hole?"

"No, but that doesn't mean it couldn't happen."

"And what about that being punished in the next world for what you've done in the past?"

"Why take chances on that either?"

The steward shook his head, "They're some insurance salesmen!"

"You see insurance salesmen," the captain said with a smile, as be put down his cup. "Personally, I see a lawyer, a general, and a priest!"

Reconciliation

It was un-nerving! Looking out the port hole, watching the amazing phenomenon, was like looking into a microscope and seeing pulsating cells swelling and dividing with jerks and snaps until masses of isomorphic objects were everywhere.

Amon Brun unconsciously shrank back, contracted his arms and pulled up his legs seeking the security of a cramped space capsule that was hurtling through space at a tremendous speed.

His compact ship had cleared the earth's atmosphere and was now unfolding like a bud bursting into flower. Geometric forms were popping out in all directions reflecting sunlight in a myriad of mirrors and shadows. New optical illusions erupted and faded. He was the center of a kaleidoscope, a strobe light, a bubble bath!

Miraculously, the growth and movement stopped with the instant precision with which it had begun. The view from the window showed the completed masterpiece. The bursting cells had become corridors and walls.

"It is unbelievable, he murmured into the radio. "The precision! The timing! From a tiny space capsule a whole honeycomb of living space has erupted!"

As he anxiously awaited the green light that would enable him to slip from the restraining belts and examine this sky scraper in space, Amon thought of the sudden and unexpected chain of events that had placed him in charge of this thrilling expedition.

Perhaps it had been the result of those anti government demonstrations in the streets, or possibly to counter the mounting adverse world opinion that he, the opposition leader, had been chosen to lead such an important exploratory mission.

Some press writers had said the administration saw the necessity for a bold new approach to the mounting problems. Somehow they must try to heal the differences among the people and to unite all the dissenting groups. There was a need to focus all attention on a united endeavor. This had certainly been done by putting the opposition leader in charge--the very leader who had been accusing them of doing nothing about the space program.

"Well, whatever the reasons, I am here," Amon said to himself. And it is important that I be successful--not only for the country, but for my party. That oppressive government must be made more enlightened. Many are wondering how I will handle this assignment, and what I will do. I certainly had a wide range of suggestions from my followers. Many of them are real militants."

A flashing green light brought Amon back to the job at hand. It was time to begin the rapid check of conditions. First he had to examine each part of this edifice by computer analysis. This meant pushing a button on the control panel for every check point in every room and corridor. It meant checking every system quickly, for the space ship with the passengers would now be leaving the earth. This traveling space city would be a bee hive of scientists and technicians in a very short time. The ingenious designers had figured a way to fold this colossus into a tiny space capsule, but had not yet mastered a method to do the same with people. So the passengers were being sent on a follow up shuttle ship.

After all the computer checks turned out positive, Amon climbed from his harness and began walking through the empty halls and rooms making his first inspection of a small part of the ship. Full inspection would have to wait. The most important thing was the docking port that must be ready to receive the shuttle.

As he looked at the docking port with its large vacant waiting room, he suddenly felt the panic of being alone. He walked to the observation window. The black velvet sky with its bright jewels and sequins whispered eternity. Those steady dots of light, looking so close, but far beyond reach, echoed endlessness.

Already he felt homesick for Earth, and yet he knew his life could never again be the same. This voyage was programmed for almost one hundred years. One hundred years to be spent charting and mapping, scooping up new knowledge that could be beamed to the great computers on Earth. And even though the life expectancy of his generation was now almost five hundred years, Amon knew that one hundred years was a lot to give up.

As Amon thought of these things great space craft was racing around the planet gathering momentum, anxious to break the tethers of gravity and leap out toward those beckoning stars. Only waiting for the arrival of the passengers delayed the ship's date with destiny.

Turning to his radio for the reassuring sound of a human voice, Amon asked, "Is the passenger rocket launch on schedule?"

The speaker was voiceless. Only silence answered him.

"Rocket Center! Rocket Center! Come in Rocket Center!"

When there was still no answer Amon checked all the switches and levers. All were glowing with a soft light. Certainly every thing was turned on. He looked anxiously at the speaker. Its open mouth was frozen and mute.

"Rocket Center! Rocket Center! Do you read me Rocket Center?" Amon shouted.

Nothing!

Following the emergency procedure, he methodically checked step by step for any possible defect in equipment. Everything seemed in order. Switching to the computer for a complete analysis of the problem, he stared in dismay as the computer reported all systems operating normally.

"Rocket Center! Rocket Center!"

The silence poured forth making his ear drums pound.

Amon rushed to the observation port and looked at distant Earth. Was it his imagination or was the earth shrinking in size? The space ship's orbit wasn't supposed to be an ellipse. The earth certainly seemed to be dropping away. Loneliness and panic paralyzed his conscious mind.

"This can't be!" he muttered. Am I going alone? Is this really happening? Am I hallucinating? Was I poisoned? The blossoming of the space craft--the kaleidoscope effect! It all seems unreal!"

As he pressed his forehead against the window and stared at the earth, his tortured mind was suddenly shocked back to reality. There was a point of light close to the earth. It wasn't a star. No, it was moving, and moving very fast. It had to be a rocket. It was growing brighter. The space shuttle!

His heart began to calm and he felt a sense of shameful anger. Then again doubt closed in. Was it indeed the space shuttle, or was it a missile? Was he to be eliminated after all?

"What am I thinking?" Amon said aloud. "Was this fantastic ship built just to eliminate one man? My ego is even more amazing than my suspicions."

He shook his head and blinked, looked away and then back to the window. Indeed there was a space ship approaching, but he must be having double vision, for two huge ships appeared side by side.

"This was not the plan. I'm sure of it. The force of the launch must have compressed my brain! I must be confused. Maybe I'm still back there strapped to my seat, and only my mind is wandering loosely around. Under pressure the mind does strange things."

Amon was completely convinced that it was his double vision that created the two ships, when suddenly one of them veered away from the other. One ship raced away while the other turned straight for the docking port. The great, bright disc approached and seemed to hang in the sky as its diameter grew larger. The silver mass totally obscured the sky, filled the window, and seemed to press against the glass. There was a gentle bump as the ship locked into the docking port.

A sweating Amon rushed to meet it. How glad he was to see the large doors part and slide open, and to see some other human beings.

"My radio isn't working," he shouted to the flight commander, who was the first to enter. "I was unable to communicate with Rocket Center."

"The radio is working. We picked up your transmission," the commander, a tall man with the name Captain Jans sewn on his shirt pocked, replied.

"Then it is not receiving. I could hear nothing," Amon continued.

"The earth was not communicating with you, but don't concern yourself with that now. We have technicians trained to handle all equipment. This flying city seems ready to receive its passengers."

"The computer analysis has indicated everything is ready," Amon assured him. "It is a magnificent craft. We can all look forward to a comfortable voyage."

"It is a marvel, and should serve our purposes well," Captain Jans agreed.

"Would you care to make a first hand inspection with me?" Amon asked. "I haven't checked the rooms."

"I would like to, but it will have to wait," Captain Jans said quickly. We are already leaving our orbit around the earth and moving into space. There is barely enough time to unload the passengers and cast off the shuttle."

The first dozen men and women to disembark wore the dark, form fitting uniforms of the national security forces. Each carried a notebook as he took his place in line. In facts the forces formed two lines between which the other passengers passed.

"The government doesn't trust space travelers any more than it trusts its citizens at home," Amon said to himself.

More than one hundred men and women, each carrying a suitcase or duffle bag, filed between the lines of security men and into the great waiting room. As the last one cleared the entrance, the great sliding doors quickly shut. The roar of the motors announced the hasty departure of the shuttle craft.

With disciplined precision a tall blond security guard strode over to Amon and, introduced himself.

"I'm Captain Oso, in charge of passengers. Shall we inspect the rooms so we may get everyone settled?"

"An excellent idea," Amon agreed. "We can have an orientation meeting later. The staterooms should be down the corridor to the left."

Without another word, Captain Oso led the way, quickly eating up the distance with his long stride. When he reached the corridor a large metal door automatically slid open.

Amon followed, running to keep up with the captain. However, as he walked through the doorway he stopped dead and stared in amazement. As he studied the room he became aware that Captain Oso was staring at him.

Then Amon turned to face him.

"When I was on this ship alone, I watched for your approach. I thought I saw two space crafts side by side. Just before you reached the dock the other ship seemed to go off into space."

Captain Oso nodded.

"That other ship," Amon asked, "was it on an exploratory mission?"

Again Captain Oso nodded and then waved Amon forward into the room ahead.

On each side of them were rows and rows, not of state-rooms, but of barred cells. And on each iron door there was a name plate.

On the very first one was the name AMON BRUN.

Who Has Escaped?

"Obviously these people are very primitive," Mac said. "For a planet a billion years older than the earth the rate of evolution has been incredibly slow."

"What did you find out there, a bunch of savages?" the commander asked.

"Mac's exaggerating a little I think," John insisted. "They aren't really primitive, at least not in the sense that they're running around with spears and using stone tools. They just seem sort of simple."

"John's right," Mac agreed. "I didn't mean primitive in a strict way. Maybe simple is a better word. They stood around in white, short robes with dismayed looks on their faces. It was as if they were dazed. I don't think they've ever seen anything like a space ship and seem to have no understanding of our arrival."

"I got the same feeling," John nodded. "Only things seemed a little weird. They weren't in awe of us and didn't try to worship us as gods the way other primitive people have done."

"I thought it was funny that they didn't act surprised when we told them we came from the planet Earth. They nodded like they understood what we were talking about. How could that have an meaning to them when they're so simple?"

"That seemed strange to me too," Mac said. "However, I think they just didn't understand. The word earth may have some other meaning. I think it was just a matter of semantics."

The three men were meeting in the control room of the space ship. Outside, the green grass still sparkled with the morning dew and the sky above this remote plateau glowed with a brilliant blue-green color. The tops of the few trees visible in the distance were gilded by this planet's dazzling sun, a sun that had turned the patches of bare ground to a blinding gold.

Commander Jacobs sat listening to the reports of Mac and John. With some irritation he suddenly stood up and waved his hand.

"Stop the speculation and let's get down to facts. You were gone over an hour! What exactly happened when you approached these people? What did they say?"

"First," Mac answered, "they wanted to know where we were from. I told them we had come in a space ship from the planet Earth."

"That," interrupted John, "was when they began acting strange. They fidgeted and looked at each other. Then one, who seemed to be a leader, asked a very unusual question."

"How did you escape?" Mac added. "Don't you think that's an odd question?"

"I think there was some mix-up in the meaning," John continued. "They really didn't comprehend what we were saying. There was no sign of an advanced technological culture. The houses here are simple, made of timber and stone. There are no roads, just dirt trails."

"I don't think you would get a question like that from a scientific community," Commander Jacobs agreed. "Maybe our data about this place is wrong. Once in a while a planet with all the right qualifications doesn't evolve as rapidly as we suppose and our estimates are wrong."

"That's what I think," John nodded. "They don't seem to have the understanding that a rocket can escape from a planet's gravity."

"It is puzzling," the commander said, thoughtfully. "Why wouldn't they ask, 'What is Earth?' or 'Where is Earth?' Of course they could know of some place called earth. Maybe it's their word for prison. They'd be surprised if we escaped from there."

"In that case they'll be wanting to capture us," Mac said.

"Until we know more about what we're dealing with here, we'd better not take any chances," the commander said. "We'll go everywhere armed and we'll stay close together. If these people are as backward as you men believe, we shouldn't have much trouble handling any situation. Remember on satellite Twelve how easily we ended all native resistance by firing our weapons at the mountain?"

"Do you want to talk with these people yourself, Commander?" John asked. "Maybe we can learn more if we engage them in some conversation. It seems to me our preliminary contact was too brief."

"Lead the way!" the commander agreed. "We don't want to turn a simple survey mission into a full blown mystery. Let's wrap this project up and get on with the schedule."

From the air the green meadow looked as if it were filled with giant flowers, but as the shuttle descended the spacemen saw the masses of color turning into smiling men and women dressed in beautiful pastel robes.

As the men left the shuttle, the people began waving and throwing flowers. Then they all were smiling and singing. The voices were soft and the music was like the whispers of baby breezes rustling the tree leaves.

In spite of his determination to stay on his guard and to keep alert, Commander Jacobs felt his tensions relaxing. The balmy summer day, the soft music, the flowers, the trees and those simple, smiling faces all suggested peace and tranquility. Certainly there was no feeling of hostility here.

Stepping forward, the commander raised his hand in peace and introduced himself.

"Although you are welcome to our humble planet," a man said as he stepped forward from the group, "we are wondering why you have come here. Are you lost? Do you need provisions? Can we give you directions?"

"No, we are not lost, and we have ample provisions. This is our intended destination. We are explorers from the planet Earth. We wish to know how you live here and to make friends."

"But, how did you escape from Earth?"

"With our rocket ship. See, it is resting on that plateau over there. The ship can go anywhere in space."

"Did you build the rocket ship?"

"The men of Earth built it. They designed and built it so we could visit other worlds."

"And you have been visiting other planets?"

"Of course. There have been many space missions by the men of Earth. Our ships have explored distant places."

"That is amazing!" The man shook his head in wonder.

"Do you understand the things I'm telling you?" the commander asked. "Do you know what a planet is?"

"Oh, yes. There are many among the countless lights in the sky."

"Each world is like this one," the commander explained, doubting his listener's comprehension. "Many have people on them."

"I know. How many have you visited, Commander?"

"Three planets and three satellites," Commander Jacobs answered proudly.

"I have been to seven planets," the man answered. "At least this is my seventh."

"You have been to seven of those worlds in the sky? The ones we've been talking about?" A tone of disbelief crept into Commander Jacob's voice.

Choosing not to notice this skepticism, the man continued, "Two of the planets were in this galaxy, but five were in the Andromeda."

"The Andromeda galaxy? That's impossible to reach!" Commander Jacobs shouted.

Looking alarmed and uneasy, and fearing an argument, the man stepped cautiously backward. He looked anxiously toward the rest of his people seeking support.

Sensing the tension, a group of girls danced forward.

Singing and smiling they handed each of the visitors a fragrant bunch of flowers.

Thanking these friendly hosts, the spacemen took the offering and withdrew a few steps.

"Perhaps we can talk more this evening," the commander suggested.

"Excellent! Let us meet here at the rising of the tri-moons," the man agreed. He then waved, smiled, and finally bowed before joining the others who were melting back among the trees.

The three spacemen, without turning their backs or taking their eyes from the assembled natives, retreated to their shuttle craft. As they blasted away up into the sky they felt as if confusing thoughts were pursuing them; like a pack of wolves snapping at their logical minds.

"It's weird! Like I said before," Mac said, "they seem to know a lot of things, but there's no evidence of anything modern. Do you think everything is hidden?"

"It could be a false front to fool visitors like us," John suggested.

"But why?" Mac asked. "Do you think they've been attacked from space? None of the other people we've visited seemed concerned about that."

"It could be they're afraid, or on the other hand they could be the hostile ones themselves," Mac said. "This could be a trap to throw us off guard."

"There could be a less sinister explanation," Commander Jacobs said. "They may be doing some exploratory research themselves. This could be a temporary base, perhaps even a secret one, for some distant civilization."

"Distant is right John agreed. "If they're from the Andromeda galaxy they have mastered an ability to travel that far exceeds our technology."

"That could help to explain their surprise at our having escaped from Earth," the commander said. "They probably know that Earth is a billion years younger than this planet. Maybe we, on Earth, have evolved unusually fast."

"Commander, if there's a possibility that they're more advanced than Earth and are playing games with us shouldn't we withdraw and make a report?" John suggested.

"No, not yet. We're not really sure about anything and my curiosity is too great to leave now. It can't be any more dangerous to stay than to try to leave now. If they are as advanced as we suppose, they could stop us if they wanted to. There is a good chance they are as harmless as they appear. We'll meet them at rising of the tri-moons and hope our weapons will provide sufficient protection."

Forming a perfect equilateral triangle in the sky, the three moons rose rapidly above the southern horizon. The three satellites were almost identical in size and hung in the sky like massive spotlights that illuminated the landscape and drove the darkness into the shadows of the trees. The scenery was done in a new palette of colors, as purples, grays and blues laced with silver replaced the green and gold of a few hours before.

The spacemen looked down at this unreal scene and it filled their hearts with a sinister foreboding. They were descending onto a silent stage where ghostly figures in white robes were standing around like pieces of sculpture in a garden of trees.

When the shuttle landed in the small meadow it was immediately surrounded by quiet people with somber faces whose eyes were reflecting the three moons. Even the tree leaves were silent as the air was holding its breath.

To break the spell, the commander called out, "We have returned as agreed, although I am not sure we are communicating."

"Perhaps in time," a voice answered from near by.

"Soon, I hope. For we don't have much time," the commander said. "Our systems are limited and we must return to Earth again."

"That is too bad. Will you be staying there long?"

"It is my home and I expect to spend most of my time there," the commander answered. "Earth is a wonderful place. We have made great scientific advancements. We have expanded the human life span by hundreds of years. We are approaching a period of eternal life."

A buzz of subdued conversation arose from the shadows, and then a voice continued. "Are the nations of Earth still having wars? Is there still racial and religious violence and intolerance?"

"We have some problems, but we are making progress. How do you know these things? Have some of your people visited Earth?"

"Oh, no, no! Never have we been to Earth or any of the nine planets of that solar system," the voice said.

Mac turned to the commander "I think they're reading our minds. They must have some extra sensory ability."

The voice from the trees called out again, "It must be terrible on Earth. People are killing, stealing, robbing and cheating. There is so much greed. Even the leaders are corrupt."

"Oh, it's not as bad as all that," John interrupted. "We have good people there too."

"Sometimes the people who do good also do harm," the voice added.

"Well, nobody's perfect," Mac said indignantly. "Where do you get your information, from some space commentator?"

"You've been asking us questions," Commander Jacobs said, "now let's talk about you. Where do you come from?"

"We come from many places and will eventually go to many places."

"Even the Andromeda galaxy?" the commander asked.

"Yes, and far beyond."

"If you come from so far, it must have taken a long time. How old are you?" Mac asked.

The answer came back in a soft chorus as if the leaves were being shuffled in the branches of the trees, "We are all eternal!"

"How did you get here? We haven't seen your ships."

"We were born here."

"If you travel to Andromeda from here you must have some amazing technology," the commander said.

"They think we travel there and back," a voice said.

"And they think we've mastered some technology," another spoke up.

"And have ships!" some others said, laughing.

"Don't you use space ships?" Commander Jacobs shouted above the voices.

"They can never be efficient," the leader said.

"Then how do you get to Andromeda? I don't understand."

"Of course you don't. You're from Earth!"

A hushed voice from far away whispered, "They don't know."

"They never do," another said.

Many conversations started all around as the shadowy figures seemed to forget the spacemen and to start talking among themselves.

"I hear things are getting worse on Earth. There are now billions of people there."

"And they are inhabiting other planets. Even additional solar systems are being placed on stand by."

"It doesn't sound as if all that theory is working."

"Silence!" Commander Jacobs shouted in irritation. "I think I'm having a nightmare! What are all you jabbering about?"

His impulsive command produced an immediate reaction. Like birds scattering from the trees when a predator approaches, the ghostly figures flew off in all directions. Only one brave leader remained and stepped out into the light.

"That violence, he exclaimed, "is why you are on Earth! Everyone here is bound to be edgy."

"You asked how we got to Andromeda," the man continued, "we were born there. We are reborn eternally and live on many planets."

"Now I get it," Mac said. "You're some strange religious sect---probably isolated here."

"You from Earth, I'm sure, believe many things, and you must stay there until you are cured. I understand some people spend many lifetimes there before they reach a spiritual level."

"Well, you can believe whatever you want," the commander said, "and you have some strange ideas. You claim to remember living other lives on other planets--even in far off Andromeda. Well, I don't remember leading any other life and neither does Mac or John. In fact I don't know anyone who remembers living on another planet."

"Anyone on Earth," the man added.

"Certainly! On Earth!"

"You see!" the man exclaimed. "That's why you are all there. All of you on Earth! It's the asylum for the universe!"

Finale

It didn't happen exactly the way everyone thought it would, and certainly it wasn't in the manner predicted. There was no glorious flash of light to herald this event to unknown watchers on distant worlds, and there was not the usual screaming newspaper headlines relaying a step by step account of the event. Actually no one noticed--that is until Homer Jones stood one morning before his bathroom mirror preparing to shave and was suddenly stunned by the truth.

As he stared critically and analytically at the image reflected back at him, he was dazed to realize that a momentous event had passed without even a comment from anyone.

"During the past fifty years," he said to himself, "I've had every organ within my body replaced with new plastic developments. I've had complete transfusions of the new super blood and received injections of synthetic hormones to regulate my emotions and expand my brain cells. But even before that my parents, after a genetic analysis, had many of their genes replaced and their hereditary codes unscrambled and reorganized.

"So I'm a superior being! Of course all of my friends and everyone else have gone through this same process. Therefore, in relation to others I'm not superior. I'm really only average. However, I am certainly superior to all previous generations! We finally got rid of the internal enemy! Man the predator is gone. Man the emotional animal is gone. That sickly creature man is gone--the creature with such a short life span.

"Homo Sapiens is extinct. He became extinct and no one even noticed. What a joke! After all the predictions of nuclear holocausts and a blazing death by fire!

"I wonder who the last man was? We'll never know, and I guess it doesn't matter. The fact is, 'Man is extinct.' And God knows, there's no one to mourn his passing!"

Visions from the Past

The Watch

She had always dreaded these days. Seeing them coming was like watching a distant fog bank moving swiftly across the water, threatening the coast land, finally blotting out the sun. What she had feared most was happening, and she was powerless to change a single thing.

He was being sent into combat. Hans was being shipped off to the Italian front.

The war had dragged on and on. The quick victories in Poland and France had not brought the anticipated end to hostilities. The British had continued the war and the Russians, aided by the terrible winter, had not succumbed as expected.

The Americans too were in the conflict. They had joined the British in Africa and destroyed Germany's pride, the Afrika Corps. Those two armies had successfully invaded Italy and were marching up the Italian boot. Every kilometer gained brought the allied airplanes closer to the homeland. So of course, it was inevitable that young Hans would be thrown into the conflagration. Germany needed every soldier to fight.

Day after day Anna had hoped for some miracle that would end the war before Hans was taken from her, but things were not to be as she wished.

One morning Hans ran up to her excited and smiling, waving a paper in his hand. These orders to report for combat duty did not frighten or depress him. There was an air of adventure to it all, although he felt sad at the thought of being away from Anna.

When she broke down and wept, he put a finger under her chin, lifted her tear streaked face, gently kissed her lips and told her to be brave.

Tomorrow Hans would be boarding the train with all the other young men in their field gray uniforms, and Anna wanted to cling to him, to go with him and to spend every last minute by his side.

"I must give him something to treasure," she said. "Some thing personal that he will keep close to him and remind him always of me. It will be a bond between us to hold onto until we are together once more."

It was then that Anna thought of just the present to give Hans. There were so few things a soldier could use or carry with him, but one thing Hans did not have was a watch. She would take her extra money and buy him a good Swiss watch, and she would have both of their initials engraved on the back.

H.W. for him and A.S. for her.

Anna had much to do and very little time, but she could be very efficient. When it was time to walk to the train station with Hans she had her precious gift tucked down inside her purse.

Just before he said his final goodbye she grabbed his hand, and after showing him the initials on the case, fastened the watch to his wrist. As she expected, Hans was overwhelmed with emotion.

"Oh, Anna," he said, "you shouldn't have done this. It looks expensive. It may get broken in the war. Maybe you should keep it for me."

"No, no," Anna shook her head. "Wear it. If you are careful of it, you will be careful of yourself. And you will bring it back safely I know."

Shortly after that Hans was gone, lost among the faces in the windows of the train, and Anna felt alone among the crowds of men and women waving goodbye.

"Hans, you're probably congratulating yourself on being sent here to the Italian front. The big news is the Eastern front in Russia and fighting back the invasion in France, but let me warn you there is a war going on here. Der Fuehrer is determined to save Italy for our ally Mussolini. That's why General Kesslering is in charge here."

The soldier talking was slouched back in his chair and his uniform was not as fresh and neat as most of the German soldiers. His face too was dry, tan and a little wrinkled from long exposure to living in the field.

"I've been in Poland and a long time on the Eastern front," he continued. "Yes,' he nodded, "I've been in this war from the beginning. And I can tell you the artillery is worse here. Day and night the shells fall. After the shells, the Americans come, pushing on, pushing on relentlessly. And we fall back."

"But now we will stop them," Hans said. "The orientation officer said we have completed the Gothic line. The Americans and British won't get through that."

"There have been other lines. Casino. Anzio," the veteran said with skepticism.

"This one is in the mountains. They won't get through to the Po valley," Hans insisted. "We will hold them until the super weapons are ready."

"Then we win the war," the older soldier added.

"Of course," Hans snapped.

"Perhaps," the veteran said, ending the discussion.

When Hans arrived with his company in the high Appenine mountains, the summer was changing to autumn and there was a chill in the mountain air. Looking to the south he could see dark mountain ridges with lighter ridges behind them. There were even lighter colored ridges beyond those. There were mountains and more mountains fading off into the sky.

Later, in the dark, moonless night his company was taken along a dirt road among those hills and peaks. Soon the men were hearing exploding artillery shells ahead, so they left the trucks and walked on. It was so dark Hans had to keep his hand on the shoulder of the soldier ahead of him in order not to lose his way.

Occasionally they heard rifle or machine gun fire from some strange mountain ridge ahead, obscured from vision by the black night. Finally they stopped by a farmhouse and dug slit trenches all around it.

The next day everything was quiet. They dug better defensive positions and their, company commander, a captain, set up head quarters in the main building.

The farm house was large with thick adobe walls that had been plastered and white washed. The first floor, which was half below ground level like a basement, was the barn for a herd of dairy cows, but the Italians had taken the cows away.

Above the barn area were two more floors of living rooms. The entire building was three stories high--an impressive size. The structure was crowned with a red tile roof.

There was a large Italian family living at the farm, so the captain had locked them all in one bedroom on the third floor to keep them out of the way, for he was sure the Americans would be coming soon.

All day and all night Hans and his company waited. There were reports that the Americans were in the farm on the next hill, so occasionally the Germans fired a machine gun in that direction. That evening a fog settled on the area and remained all night.

With the first gray light of dawn the action began as machine gun fire raked their area. The Americans had moved up with the fog in the night and were on the slope of the hill directly in front and to the left of the house.

Hans and his buddies crouched low in their slit trenches and returned the fire.

Suddenly there was a series of explosions. Hand grenades were being lobbed into the German positions. The Americans were very close, so some of the Germans began flipping their own grenades. Looking like potato mashers, these whipped end over end toward the attackers. The firing grew intense.

The sun was rising high into the sky. Both sides continued rifle and machine gun fire, but the Americans did not advance.

"I think we outnumber them," the captain said. "They are afraid to attack. And they can't withdraw across the fields. We would cut them to pieces."

Intermittent firing continued for several hours and then an American called out in German that he would like to talk to the defenders.

The firing ceased. The American soldier stood up and told the Germans that their war was lost. In order to save lives they should surrender.

"Your position is hopeless," a German officer yelled back. "It is you who should surrender."

The American position was indeed difficult, but they did not agree with the German officer and soon the firing continued.

The German captain ordered mortars brought up.

"We can get them with these," he said. "The hillside will be no protection now."

First he ordered smoke rounds fired so they could see where the shells were landing. When the smoke plumes rose beyond the Americans, he ordered a small adjustment in the angle of fire.

It was obvious that the mortar shells could easily hit the American positions. The Americans could take this devastating punishment, they could pull back and be shot to pieces as they crossed the plain to the rear, or they could surrender.

Suddenly there was panic and confusion everywhere American soldiers were running all through the area throwing hand grenades and firing in all directions. The exploding grenades thundering of automatic weapons and loud yelling created the panic and chaos.

Some of Han's buddies began to run around behind the farm house, but Americans were running there too. Other German soldiers took off running up the hill to their rear. Before they knew what was happening, Hans and about forty others were surrounded. Even the captain was surprised and found himself a prisoner.

There were dead, wounded and dying soldiers all around the house. Casualties were heavy on both sides.

Hans and the other prisoners were herded into a room where the hay was stored. A group of Americans frisked them, checking their identification cards and wallets, taking their jewelry and especially their watches. In a flash Hans saw his prized watch snatched from his wrist and disappear.

The American soldiers left and Hans and the other German soldiers sat down in the hay. An American guard was outside the door, which was tightly closed. Through the only small window they could see another American guard.

Hans was quietly thinking of Anna and his home when four violent explosions shattered the room. Beams and thatching from the roof were crashing to the floor and smoke was whirling around. The door had been blown open and the Germans were stampeding out screaming. Four heavy German mortar shells had hit the room in which the prisoners were waiting. The enemy was striking back.

The American guard motioned for the panic stricken Germans to go into the basement room where there were stalls for the dairy cows. The wounded German prisoners were carried into this stable and laid on the dirt floor. Several of the prisoners had been killed and many were badly wounded. Hans felt very lucky that he was unhurt.

All day and all night the prisoners and the three American guards stayed together while the shells fell all around the house. Many of wounded Germans were calling for water and a few were delirious.

The second morning the Americans decided to pull back, and all the prisoners who were able to walk were ordered to go along with them. Hans followed the others, walking along with both hands resting on the top of his head. It was several kilometers to where the trucks were waiting to take them to a prisoner of war camp.

Bill Cooper looked at the watch carefully. He studied the engraved initials H.W. and A.S. They meant nothing to him. It looked like a good watch, and he didn't have one. The wrist band fit him very well.

"Spoils of war," he said to himself. "Those Krauts killed my buddies. The one who lost this was lucky it was all he lost."

Bill Cooper was a rifleman, and like the other soldiers in his squad he carried an M-1 rifle, two bandoliers of ammunition and two hand grenades that hung from the shoulder straps of his light pack. He also carried two canteens on his belt, for water was often hard to find.

He no longer carried a gas mask, but inside his wool shirt next to his chest were two small box rations. He wanted to travel light so he could run and dive for cover without being bogged down with a lot of bothersome equipment. Buttoned inside his shirt pocket was a New Testament, a spoon and a razor, which he rarely had time, or water enough, to use.

His age was average for his platoon, nineteen.

Bill had been in the army for a year and a half and had five months of combat experience. This was the third week of fighting in the Gothic line, and the mountains ahead seemed endless.

After the battle for the farmhouse in which Hans had been captured, Bill's company was ordered to move to another sector where the battle for a key mountain position was beginning.

"If we don't break into the Po Valley before winter," his company commander said, "we'll be stuck in these damn mountains until spring--stuck in the snow and blizzards. A hell of a way to spend New Years!"

One of the first objectives was to secure a mountain pass with a paved highway running through it. Bill's company moved along the mountain ridge above the pass while a battalion opened an attack through the valley below.

At first the battle went well for the Americans. Advancing with tanks and artillery fire they moved slowly forward. High on the ridge the company moved forward also, encountering light machine gun and occasional rifle fire.

Later in the day, however, the Germans counter attacked heavily and the American companies fell back to consolidate their positions in the pass. Since Bill's company did not pull back, Bill and the others in his platoon found themselves isolated on the ridge. With night coming on they had no sure knowledge of how far the Germans had advanced on their flanks. The company could be cut off, or even surrounded.

Such a precarious position called for unusual actions. The captain in command ordered the men to set up defensive positions along the trail. Half of the company was to remain awake at all times. Everyone would have an hour asleep and an hour awake all night, alternating with a buddy.

Around the perimeter of the company position special out-posts were set up. Bill's squad was to man one of these. Two men were to man the outpost for two hours and then awaken two more men to relieve them. These two hour shifts would go on all night.

"We'll need a watch with a luminous dial to keep track of the time," the sergeant said. "Does anyone have one?"

No one spoke up so Bill held up his recent acquisition.

"I have one."

"O.K.," the sergeant said, "give it to Martin and Smith. They'll take the first shift. They'll wake up their replacements in two hours and pass the watch on. Remember! When you wake up your replacement, give him the watch."

Bill was sleeping soundly when he felt someone shaking his arm. Hating to leave the world of sleep and face the desperate reality, he wanted to ignore this interruption, but it was futile to resist.

"Hey, Bill, it's time for outpost," the whispered voice in the night persisted.

"O.K., O.K.," Bill nodded, sitting up.

Soon he was crouched in a shallow slit trench listening to distant night sounds and shivering in the cool damp air. He peered intently all around, but it was like looking at a black wall. Even the sky was starless and dark.

Looking down at his watch, he saw the only light in his universe, those familiar numerals glowing faintly. He felt a sudden kinship for them. They were comforting and rational in this alien, irrational environment.

It took a long time for those hands to advance. The night was long and slow in passing. The watch said one o'clock, then one ten, one fourteen, one seventeen. Would the hands never get to two? And after two they had to move on to three. The night was cold and dark, but also it was quiet. The Germans too were dug in, watching and waiting.

In the early morning the company moved on. The weather was gray, looking like it could rain at any time. The trail climbed up higher and higher along the side of the mountain. The men were tired, but said nothing as they put more effort into climbing the steep path.

Near the top the ground leveled off more until it was a gentle slope. Several mortar shells exploded ahead, so the order was given to stop and dig two men slit trenches. A reconnaissance patrol would be sent ahead.

Bill, with his buddy, Art Basset, dug a temporary home in the damp soil. Their slit trench was the usual size, about six feet long, three feet wide and four feet deep. When it was finished they both climbed in, sitting at opposite ends facing each other. A slight mist was falling, so Art took a canvas shelter half that he carried folded over his belt and spread it across the top of the hole.

Soon they heard some more mortar shells exploding ahead, and then one much closer. After that a voice called out.

"We need help. Help to carry a guy who's been hit!"

"Let's go help them," Bill said, rising and climbing out of the slit trench.

Art nodded and followed his buddy.

A great hand slapped them both down. As they hit the ground they heard a great booming sound and the air was filled with acrid smoke.

Art looked over at Bill, who had been hurled a few feet away. There were blood marks on his chest. Staggering to his feet, he rushed over to his buddy and yelled for a medic.

Pierson, the platoon medic was there at once. Bill was lying still, breathing heavily. After opening Bill's shirt and checking the wounds, Pierson yelled for litter bearers.

"We'll have to get him to the aid station at once," he said to Art.

As they lifted him onto the stretcher, Bill feebly grabbed Art's arm.

"Take the watch," he said. "You'll need it on outpost." Art nodded, with tears in his eyes.

"You'll be O.K. I'll keep it for you."

The medics were half running as they carried Bill away. Art called after them, "I'll see you soon."

Art Basset was a sergeant and the squad leader for the third squad in the second platoon of B company. There were twelve men in his squad including a three man automatic rifle team and a two man bazooka team. He had been in charge for over two months, having been promoted when the previous leader had been killed.

The day after Bill had been hit, B company was ordered to advance once more, and again the direction was forward and up. They climbed through large boulders up to a small plateau that was the crest of the mountain.

"Have your men dig in here and hold this position," the lieutenant said. He then took the rest of the company and moved off to another part of the mountain.

Quickly the men in the squad began digging. The fog was creeping across the land, moving toward them like a curtain.

"We're up in the clouds," Martin said.

"Too bad you can't drink 'em," Smith said. "This digging's tough. Do you have any water left in your canteen?"

Martin didn't have a chance to answer. A deafening clatter shattered the stillness. Spots of light were flying everywhere from out of the fog. One machine gun, then another, and then a third one sprayed the area with tracer bullets.

It was quickly over! Every man in the squad lay dead--every man but one! Art Basset lay still, sprawled on the ground, shot in the leg. Dark figures were emerging from the fog. German soldiers walked through the area checking the bodies.

One bent over Art and rolled him over. Art froze and prayed to himself. The German said something to a buddy and went on.

Art lay still for a long time, then cautiously opened his eyes. Through the dense fog he could see the still, lifeless bodies of his men frozen in the grotesque shapes in which they had fallen, some with their small shovels still in their hands, some reaching up toward the sky as they lay on their backs. One had a serene smile on his face.

Rolling his eyes to look the other way, he could see the shadowy form of a machine gun and two figures who were walking around, about ten feet away.

Art could hear voices speaking German and he could feel the sharp pain from the wound in his leg.

"I must not moan. I must not move," he told himself.

Soon the German soldiers were walking once more among the bodies. This time they were stripping things of value from them and gathering up the canteens. One soldier bent over Art, unfastened his canteen and took his wallet and the watch from his wrist.

All day and all night Art lay still. His leg throbbed with pain, but he kept his mind on the reasons he must live, his wife and home, his family waiting and praying for his safety.

The following morning the fog was as heavy as before. He could hardly see the Germans. His mind was beginning to play tricks. Phantom figures were among the bodies of his comrades. Was he going mad?

The phantoms were coming toward him, running silently.

Americans! They were American soldiers. He must warn them!

"Over here......over here," he kept saying, half aloud, but fearing the Jerries might hear him.

The misty figures had seen the dead bodies and were be coming cautious. Only a couple of men were still advancing, moving silently, listening and peering anxiously into the fog.

As one passed by, Art took a chance and called softly from his fallen position, "Over here!"

Immediately a sergeant was leaning down beside him.

"It's a trap," Art whispered, talking rapidly. "Machine guns all over....my squad was wiped out. I'm hit in the leg...can't walk, been playing dead since yesterday. Get back. It's a death trap."

The metallic snap of a machine gun bolt sent the sergeant scurrying. The firing started again and the phantom figures were diving and fleeing in all directions.

Since the Americans could not see the enemy in the fog, they did not fight back. The afternoon and evening passed in silence with no more action.

Soon it was dark once more. Art listened to the noises of the night and from the German area he heard muffled sounds. These noises grew fainter and farther away and finally faded out. The night was intensely quiet, but tension radiated from all directions.

At the dawn the fog vanished with the darkness, and with the rising sun the Americans closed in from three directions, storming across the mountain top. However, there was no firing or fighting, for the Germans had slipped away.

As the medics carried Art back on a stretcher, he told the story of the massacre of his men.

The watch lay safely in the pocket of Eric's tunic. He didn't need it. He had a good watch already. However, he could trade it for something when he got the chance.

This was an opportunity that didn't come. When the German machine gunners pulled back, Eric was the last to go. When he received the order to withdraw with absolute silence, most of the others had already gone. By the time he got his gear together he was completely alone.

Eric couldn't see a thing in the darkness and fog, and although he was fairly certain of the direction the others had gone, he was uncertain about the trail. Stumbling along among low bushes, he suddenly felt the ground slip under his foot. Pitching sideways, he was hurtling and rolling down an embankment. When he stopped rolling he felt the intense pain in his leg that told him it was broken. His other ankle seemed sprained, and his ribs ached.

The order had been given to remain silent under all circumstances, but Eric desperately needed assistance. After some thought he decided to call for help. He knew his comrades were getting farther away every minute.

He called out, but received no answer. He called twice more, each time a little louder. There was no response.

There were cracking and snapping sounds in the brush. Some one was nearby.

Again Eric called out, "Hilfe!"

"It's from over there," a voice said in English.

"Oh...," Eric moaned.

"Here he is! It's a Kraut," the voice said as an American soldier bent over him.

Soon there, were Americans all around him. Eric did not speak English, but managed to let them know that he was injured and needed help.

"It's an injured Kraut," an American shouted. "Come on, somebody. Help carry him out of here."

Five soldiers carried Eric to a hillside where a whole company of Americans had gathered. The pain was so great that he had almost lost consciousness when they carried him up.

"We'll have to get him to an aid station," a medic said.

"That means carrying him on a stretcher for three or more miles," the sergeant said. "After what happened here I won't ask anyone to do it, but if there are any volunteers, go ahead."

Four soldiers walked over to the medic and soon Eric was being lifted onto a litter. It was a jarring ride with the men stumbling through the brush as they picked their way across the rough mountain terrain in the black of night. Each jerk of the litter sent a piercing pain through his entire body. He often thought he could bear it no longer.

Since he did not speak English and his captors spoke no German, Eric tried the language with which both armies had had frequent contact.

"Quanta kilometer?" he kept asking.

"Uno," the Americans always answered.

The aid station was a small room in a dark farmhouse. Although the building looked deserted from the outside, there was warmth and activity inside. By the light from burning candles and the glow of the fire in the fireplace the injured German and the Americans who had carried him could see each others faces for the first time.

The light also disclosed the pained look in Eric's eyes.

A medic examined him briefly and then gave him a lit cigarette.

"Danke," Eric mumbled, placing it between his lips and puffing silently.

The four American litter bearers talked briefly with the medic and prepared to leave. Eric reached out and grabbed one by the arm. Then, putting his hand deep into his tunic he drew out the watch. With a painful effort he placed it in the soldier's hand.

The American gave him a quizzical look, examined the watch briefly and then handed it back to him.

Eric shook his head and would not take it.

"We've got to get back," someone said.

The soldier nodded a thanks to Eric and stuffed the watch into his pocket. He then turned abruptly and followed the others out into the night.

As he stumbled along the dark trail back to his company area, Jerry Nelson thought about the captured Kraut. He didn't know why he had volunteered to carry him, but even though he was tired he felt a deep satisfaction from having done something humane. Jerry hated the war and the terrible things that people were doing to each other.

When he was growing up he couldn't stand to see even an animal hurt or suffering.

His company had captured Krauts before and he noticed that after an enemy had surrendered and taken off his helmet he looked just like some G.I. Often a prisoner would pull out pictures of a wife and children and show them to his captors. When Jerry had asked one prisoner why he was fighting, he had answered that he was fighting because he had been drafted. Jerry could identify with that.

The four Americans finally reached their area only to find that company C had moved on. At first they felt lost, but when they found some men who were taking supplies to their company they tagged along. The supply men were glad of this also, for there was security in numbers.

Company C had assembled with the two other companies in the battalion, A and B companies. Together they were planning an assault on a high mountain that occupied a key position above the Po valley. Scouting reports indicated the Germans had machine guns and other defenses scattered around the area. The following night, under cover of darkness, A and B companies pushed off and began the climb toward the top. After encountering occasional machine gun fire that forced them to change directions several times, the two companies reached the level summit. A farmhouse and a church sat in the middle of the open yard.

The house was entered and searched. It was deserted, so the battalion commander decided a command post could be set up there. Communications men were sent for and soon two telephone linemen came walking across the yard carrying a reel of wire between them. Slowly they advanced toward the house, unreeling the wire, which lay along the ground.

Suddenly a shot rang out and one of the linemen went down.

A rifle team was quickly dispatched to search the perimeter of the yard and a nearby hay stack, but nothing was found.

When the third company, C company, arrived at the summit the night was fading and the sky was growing light. In single file the men advanced toward the house, but when they were in the open area, machine guns opened fire and mortar shells rained from the sky.

Jerry dropped to the ground and lay flat. He was in the middle of a Fourth of July display that showered burning shrapnel all around him.

At the edge of the yard was a sharp drop off where some of the men had managed to scramble out of the reach of the machine gun fire. Two sergeants yelled for Jerry to run over there. Another soldier jumped up and the machine gun opened fire and he was hit in the legs just as he went over the embankment.

The machine gun stopped firing and the sergeant yelled for Jerry to run. So, taking a deep breath, he raced for the bank. As he hurtled over it two men caught him and pulled him down. The machine gun fired again, but it was too late.

For the next five days the three companies clung to their lofty perch. A and B companies held the house and church while C company dug in on the southern slope. The Germans were entrenched on the northern side.

A cold rain fell almost continuously, but the battle grew hot. Mortar and artillery shells thundered in sporadically and machine guns fired across the summit. C company set up machine gun outposts every few feet and the men in the company took turns manning them twenty-four hours a day.

Jerry and his buddy, Preston, like the rest of the men, had dug a slit trench and stretched a canvas shelter half over the top to keep the rain out. With everyone underground, the area looked like a sea of mud. No one could tell the slit trenches from the surrounding ground, so occasionally someone on his way to an outpost would step on a shelter half and crash down on the occupants below, bringing mud and water, and receiving a barrage of swearing in return.

The artillery shells wiped out a herd of cattle grazing on an adjoining meadow, and screaming mortar shells, a Nazi terror weapon, shrieked shrilly. Five shells at a time were fired and they all streaked down with piercing screams that grew louder and louder until the five explosions jarred the area.

One evening a barrage of heavy artillery hit into the company C area. A buddy in the next slit trench was killed and Jerry and Preston were buried in an avalanche of mud.

A medic saw the disaster and heard the cry for help. With a small shovel, in the middle of the barrage, the medic dug the two men out.

Jerry sat in the rain and mud looking at his wrist. A piece of shrapnel had grazed it and it was throbbing and bleeding. Preston examined it also, and he thought the wrist might be broken.

The aid station was in the basement of the church up on the top area, and by the time Jerry and Preston reached it, Jerry's arm was swollen and aching. More shells were falling as they raced into the building.

They stood in the entry hall looking at the stairway that led down to the aid station, but before they could descend a shell hit the room in front of them. Suddenly they were looking at the rainy sky, for the ceiling and roof in front of them had collapsed. The aid station vanished in a heap of rubble as everything fell into the basement.

Jerry and Preston dropped to the floor of the only room left standing. Lying on his stomach with his hands clasped over his neck, Jerry trembled and prayed while the shells continued to fall.

"We've got to get out of the building and back to a slit trench," he said to Preston.

At the first lull in the shell fire they jumped up and ran madly out and past a well where the bodies of two dead German soldiers lay. Racing on down the slope they found a slit trench where two buddies in their squad invited them to stay.

When the devastating barrage finally ended, the medics began evacuating the many wounded men. The line of injured soldiers moved slowly down the steep mountain side and Preston told Jerry he should join the others and get some medical attention.

As Jerry made his way with the others his wrist throbbed in the cold mountain air. Putting his good hand into his pocket for warmth, he grasped the watch with his fingers.

"I forgot that was there," he said aloud. "If I'd been wearing the watch it would have been smashed to bits. It sure wouldn't have stopped a piece of shrapnel."

The game had been going on for hours and the cigarette smoke had grown dense enough to encircle the overhead light with a milky haze. The faces of the men looked tired, but their eyes were alert and darting back and forth from the cards in their hands to the pile of money on the blanket.

When the first cards were dealt there were nine men sitting or lying around the bed. The increasingly higher stakes had taken their toll and only four were still in the poker game. Jerry Nelson studied his cards carefully. His run of luck was continuing. His three tens and two jacks seemed adequate to take the pot. In this game of five card draw most of the winning hands hadn't been too impressive. Three jacks took the last one.

Evidently his main adversary had a good hand too. They had both bet and raised until Jerry's money was all in the pot. And now Bart, as everyone called him, had raised the bet another fifty.

Well, it was alright with Jerry. He'd just win more in the end. This Bart could even be bluffing. He acted like a real pro at poker. Looked like he'd been around a lot.

Although Bart, too, was a G.I. he wasn't one of the patients in the hospital ward like the other players. He had just dropped in to visit when the game started. In fact, he was the one who had suggested they get up a game.

"I can't quit now," Jerry said, "There's too much at stake." Then an idea struck him.

"Bart," he said, "I don't have the fifty, but I have this watch. It's a good one--worth more than fifty. If it's O.K. I'll bet it and call. Otherwise I'll have to hit some of my buddies here for the money. They can come up with it, but I'd rather bet the watch."

Bart put down his cigarette, exhaled a stream of smoke, and reached for the watch. He examined it carefully, turning it over several times in his hand.

"Looks good," Bart said. "It has initials on it. Those your girls?"

"No, no," Jerry shook his head. "I don't know what they're for."

"Where'd you get the watch?" Bart asked.

"From a Kraut prisoner. It's a good Swiss watch. Will it make the bet?"

"Yeh," Bart nodded. "It looks O.K."

"Well, I called you," Jerry reminded him.

"Full house," Bart said.

"I've a full house too," Jerry said.

"Three queens, two nines," Bart said, spreading the cards on the blanket.

"Damn," Jerry said. "There's hardly been a full house all night and now two in one deal. It's your pot. I'm tens and jacks."

"That's the way the ball bounces," Bart said, scooping up the money, and holding onto the watch.

"Well, that's it, I guess," Jerry said. "I'm cleaned."

The others had had enough too. Turning, they all shuffled off to their own beds.

"We'll have another game," Bart said. "Maybe you'll be the lucky one next time. I have to get back--pulling guard in the morning. Now that's a dull job, but somebody has to keep all those civilians out. This place would be full of beggars and scum selling stuff--pimps and whores too, but you probably wouldn't mind that too much! You may not know it, but this place is like an island. Naples is a jungle out there."

Once outside the large pyramidal tent that served as a hospital ward, Bart walked across the fairgrounds to the main hospital building. The American hospital occupied the entire site of what had been the planned location for Mussolini's future world's fair.

Soon Bart was through the gates and into the confusion of the streets. Oxen pulled wagons loaded with produce, and horses with bright plumes in their bridals pulled brightly painted carts. The vibrant red and gold decorations added a touch of gayety to the depressing scene. The people waved and smiled. Time seemed to stand still in Naples and the people seemed forever resilient. They accepted everything and carried on, even during this devastating war.

As he entered a plaza area with people, animals, carts and army vehicles intermingling and pushing through the maze, Bart was aware of a band of children--young teenagers, heading his way.

"Hey, G.I.," one called out. "Cigaretti, chocolate, paisan."

Now a bunch of them were yelling, holding out their hands.

Bart knew the problems. He saw this every day. Bands of orphans or displaced children roamed the streets, living in the rubble and subsisting anyway they could.

"No chocolate," he said, shaking his head. He certainly wasn't going to give them his cigarettes. He only got a limited ration himself, and here on the open market they were $1.50 a pack, American.

"Hey Joe," one said, coming closer.

Suddenly the kid grabbed Bart's arm.

Bart quickly jerked his arm away, but as he did so he saw his new watch snatched from his wrist. In a flash the boy tossed it to another and the whole band disappeared, running and ducking and weaving among the crowds.

Bart snorted and shook his head in disgust.

"That was fast! I just won the damn thing!"

"I got it! It's mine!" Mario shouted. "Why are you holding on to it? You know it's mine."

"We all got it," Antonio said calmly. "You just happened to be closer. If you hadn't grabbed it someone else would have."

"But I'm the one who got it," Mario yelled louder. "So it's mine."

"You wouldn't have got away with it if it weren't for the rest of us," Antonio insisted. "So it belongs to us all. Besides, you don't have the connections. I can get a good price for it. You'd trade it away for nothing."

"That's not fair," Mario said, looking at the other boys who were listening to the disagreement. Unfortunately, their faces weren't sympathetic. Their eyes told him his argument was futile.

"Damn it!" Mario said, stamping the dirt with his bare foot. Turning, he walked away from the others and sat by himself on a pile of stone.

Mario had not been with this group for long. He'd been staying with his aunt ever since the American bombers had leveled his home near Sorento killing both of his parents and injuring his sister. He had been the only lucky one in the house the night of the raid, although his leg had been broken and he now walked with a limp.

Since Mario had no other close relatives, he had gone to live with his aunt and her five children, but life there had been very hard. His uncle was a prisoner of war in Africa and his aunt was trying to feed her five hungry mouths and herself. There never was enough of anything, and seeing the five younger children always hungry made Mario feel guilty.

Finally he met Angelo, a boy his own age who lived in the streets and seemed to know all the tricks necessary to get what he needed from the American G.I.s.

"You run errands, take them to where the girls are, get vino for them, trade some souvenirs and sometimes find a drunk alone and roll him," Angelo said.

"I don't think I could do that," Mario said. "I don't think I could roll someone."

"Not a G.I. friend," Angelo said. "Somebody you don't know. If the guy's dead drunk and you don't take the money, somebody else will. It's survival! Everybody's the same--desperate!"

Gradually Mario drifted into the street life too. He stayed away from home for long periods of time and eventually started living with the group who lived in the rubble near the harbor in Naples.

Picking up the watch had been his first try at stealing, although he had watched Angelo pick pockets and snatch things from the open shops several times. He felt especially bad about losing the watch to Antonio, but was even more disheartened because his friend Angelo hadn't stuck up for him. During the argument Angelo had just stood silently with the other boys.

As Mario sat alone leaning against part of a cold wall feeling sorry for himself, he suddenly felt a hand on his shoulder.

"Cheer up, Mario," Antonio said, "You'll get your share. I know where I can sell the watch. I have connections. I'm in with the G.I.s. I'll bet I can get ten packs of cigarettes for it. I'll see that you get--maybe four packs. You can get anything you want for four packs. Right?

"You were pretty fast when you snatched the watch. And you have an innocent face. There'll be more watches. You'll do alright. Maybe you and your friend Angelo and I can split off from the others. Like I said, I have connections for selling the stuff."

Vic Davis looked like a soldier. He wore the uniform and he had a regular army job with the supply corps, but he was a P.B.S. (Permanent Base Station) commando, as the front line troops called him. He was a survivor, always managing to be assigned to a rear echelon job at a base station away from the fighting.

Yes, he looked like a soldier with his sharp new uniform, shiny combat boots and new field jacket, but he was really a big time operator wheeling and dealing in all kinds of merchandise, black market and otherwise. In fact his private business took so much of his time that he hardly could carry out his army duties. His supply orders were rarely filled on time, and were usually a little on the short side.

Being a sergeant, Vic Davis had a little more freedom of movement than the lower ranked enlisted men, so being the opportunist that he was, he circulated among the other rear echelon companies and got to know many of the non coms and a few of the officers. They all knew him as a guy who could get whatever they needed or wanted, even in war torn Italy.

When Antonio brought Vic the watch, he examined it carefully. He had picked up a lot of things from Antonio. In fact, Antonio had even found some hard to get items for him out in that Neapolitan jungle.

Vic could see that it was a good Swiss watch, but he knew he had to do some hard bargaining to maintain a tough reputation. Otherwise, the word would get around that he was a soft pushover.

"I don't know," he said, shaking his head. "Used watches are pretty common around here. I don't know how long I'd have to keep it before I could unload it."

"Oh, you lie," Antonio said. "Watches are scarce. There are none in the stores. Everybody wants watches."

"Yes, but they want good ones. How do I know how old this is? Does it keep time?"

"It's perfect!" Antonio said indignantly. "Muolta Buona! I can get twenty packs of cigarettes for it, but since we're friends I thought I'd give you first chance."

Vic valued his contact with Antonio, so he decided not to push things too far.

"O.K.," he said, "I'll give you ten packs, and that's twice what it's worth."

"You crazy!" Antonio howled. "Eighteen packs. I can sell it for that anywhere."

"Ten packs," Vic insisted.

"Fifteen," Antonio bargained.

"Twelve, or take it away," Vic finally said.

"O.K. twelve," Antonio agreed. "You robber!"

Vic dug into his duffle bag and counted out twelve packs of cigarettes. These were from his own P.X. ration and cost him five cents each. So the watch cost him sixty cents, unless he figured how much he could have gotten for the cigarettes. Twelve packs at one dollar and fifty cents a pack on the open market added up to eighteen dollars.

After Antonio left, Vic studied the watch again.

"Good looking piece," he said to himself.

Every day the G.I.s in Italy scanned the army newspaper, <u>Stars and Stripes</u> and every day they told the civilians "La guerra finito presto." (The war will end soon.)

The Americans were in Germany and the Russians were in Poland. The Third Reich was collapsing rapidly.

Then finally, in May the end did come. The most savage European war was finished, but the continent was a smoldering ruin.

All the G.I.s were anxious to get home, but inevitably some were assigned to army of occupation duty.

One of these unlucky soldiers was Vic Davis. His expert maneuvering couldn't save him this time. A point system had been worked out by the army, and based on time of service the ones with the most points were sent home first. Vic didn't have enough points!

When he got his orders to go to Germany while some of his buddies were going home, he felt his world was caving in.

"Man, how I envy you all," he said. "I'd give anything for a ticket on that ship."

"There's no way you can deal for that," a buddy said, "but cheer up. The war's over. You're going to a nice quiet area and I've heard the Germans are a lot like the Americans. You'll be passing the time drinking Kraut beer with a beautiful broad."

"I hope you're right," Vic said.

"Just don't trade those krauts out of what's left of their country," his buddy laughed.

Anna was drunk with happiness. Although her future was grim and the neighborhood around her was in ruins, she was dashing around with joy, for Hans was coming home. She had just received word that he would soon be arriving with a shipment of prisoners.

With the war lost and the factory where she had been working closed, she should have felt dejected like the others around her, but her love lifted her into the air like a brightly colored balloon and she could see nothing but sunshine everywhere.

Ilsa, her sister, smiled too. Seeing her sister in such a state of hysteria brought back memories of the old days--the times before the war when the family had celebrated many holidays and happy occasions together.

Now mama and papa were dead and her brother had been killed in Russia. Only Anna and Ilsa remained to greet a returning Hans.

"I always knew he would come back, Ilsa," Anna said. "When I gave him the watch he promised to bring it back to me. I always knew he would do it."

"Perhaps it was as you believed, a good luck piece. You believed it would keep him safe, and it did."

On the slow moving train Hans too was anxious. The kilometers passed slowly and the cars were often side tracked for hours before moving along again.

Seeing the shambles of German cities depressed him. He watched the burned out depots and twisted rail yards pass by. The fury of the allied bombs was visible everywhere.

Seeing such devastation made Hans worry about his own home town, but he knew that he could bear any hardships as long as Anna was still there. He could still see her sad face as she waved goodbye so long ago. She has spent her savings for the watch. What a pity that had been!

"I couldn't even save that," he thought. "We lost every thing, even Germany! I feel ashamed. How can I explain being taken prisoner? And how can I explain to Anna about the watch?"

Riding on the same train with the prisoners was a group of American soldiers. Playing cards, they watched the passing scenes of desolation without emotion.

"Now that Germany, herself, has been hit maybe the people won't be so militaristic," one said.

"Yes," Vic said. "We got what we wanted, unconditional surrender."

Vic and the others were being transferred to Germany, but they were also assigned to assist the M.P.s on the train with the transporting of the prisoners.

Vic didn't really feel any hatred for these men and boys. As he saw the anxious looks in their eyes, he knew exactly how they felt. He too would like to go home.

Finally, the train stopped at a small town and a group of prisoners was taken off. Vic envied them as he saw them march away. The other prisoners, also, watched their departing comrades. They knew their turns would be coming soon.

"Where are you from?" Vic asked the prisoner next to him.

"Near Stuttgart," the German answered in good English.

"Do you have a family there?"

"Yes, my mother and younger sister. Also my fiancé, Anna, is there."

"I'll bet you're getting nervous," Vic said. "We aren't far from Stuttgart now."

"I am," the prisoner smiled. "It will be good to see them all. And it will be hard to explain about being taken prisoner."

"They won't care," Vic said. "They'll be so happy they won't care about anything. I know how my family would feel."

"I know," the prisoner nodded, "but I feel a little ashamed. Especially I feel badly about Anna, my fiancé. When I left she spent all her savings on a watch for me and I promised to bring it back safely to her. She said she wanted that promise from me because then I'd come back safely too."

"She'll just be glad to see you back," Vic said.

"Yes, but see!" Hans held up both wrists. "No watch!"

"That's no problem," Vic said. "I sort of deal and trade around. I've been in the supply corps. in Italy for the last two years. You trade this for that and find what your buddies need. I always have a few watches on hand. Maybe we can make a deal."

"No," Hans shook his head. "I have to have the watch she gave me. It has our initials on it."

"I can get initials engraved on a watch--although it's pretty short notice. Anything's possible with the right connections. Do you have any money to buy a watch?"

"I have a little that I earned doing extra work in the camp. I do good leather work."

"Here," Vic said, "let me show you a few watches."

"It will do no good," Hans shook his head.

"Here they are," Vic said as he reached into his duffle bag and pulled out a small cloth bag.

A few seconds later he had a handful of watches spread out on the seat.

Hans looked at them with casual interest, but suddenly frowned.

"That silver one," he said. "It is a Swiss watch, ya?"

"It sure is," Vic said, picking it up. That's a good one. I got it from a boy in Italy. Traded cigarettes for it."

"It looks like the one Anna gave me. Ya, it is the same make."

"See, what did I tell you," Vic said. "We'll get some initials on it and you'll be all set."

Vic handed the watch to Hans and he looked at the face carefully. Then he turned it over and looked at Vic with disbelief.

"What's the matter?" Vic asked, looking down at the watch.

"Oh, damn it! It already has initials on it, doesn't it. I don't know if we can get those off."

"No, no," Hans shook his head. "The initials! Look! H.W. and A.S., Anna and mine! This is the watch. This is my watch, the one Anna gave me."

"That's impossible," Vic said. "How could it come back to you just like that?"

"It is my watch!"

"Well, it's my watch until you pay me for it. I bought it fair and square."

"What do you want for it?" Hans asked.

"Well, let me think now. I gave that kid cigarettes----twelve or fourteen packs. It cost me at least eighteen American dollars. What will you give me for it?"

"Twenty-five dollars," Hans said.

"That's not much of a mark up," Vic said. "Hell, I've had this watch a long time. Had my money tied up in it, not earning any interest."

"I don't have much money," Hans said.

"Well," Vic said. "Since I got it by trading cigarettes I let you have it for thirty dollars, and that's rock bottom."

"Thirty dollars," Hans said seriously and reached into his pocket. "I can just make it, but it will be worth it for Anna."

"Oh, hell! Twenty-five," Vic said.

When the train stopped and Hans marched off with the others, Vic watched him from the train. The M.P.s carried a clip board with lists of names. They checked Hans off, and at last he was free.

As he looked anxiously around, he didn't even notice all the rubble, for his eyes were searching through the crowd of civilians that had formed.

"Hans!" a voice called. "Hans!"

There she was, struggling to reach him. Anna was radiant.

"Oh, Hans," she gasped as he drew her toward him in a tight embrace. "Now things will be good again."

Pulling him by the hand she led him through the crowd and away from the people. Then, stopping, she took his hand in both of hers and clasped it to her bosom. The watch flashed in the sunlight!

"I knew it," Anna said. "I knew it would bring you back safely to me!"